Poetic Rapture

NOVEL ONE OF
THE GENTLE DOMINANT SERIES

Also by the same author

The Gentle Dominant

J. L. Thomas

Poetic Rapture

Chimera

A CIP catalogue record for this title is
available from the British Library.

ISBN 978 1 903 1365 60

Chimera is an imprint of
Pegasus Elliot MacKenzie Publishers Ltd.
www.pegasuspublishers.com

First Published in 2017

Chimera
Sheraton House Castle Park
Cambridge England

Printed & Bound in Great Britain

For: Darius

PRELUDE

As my warm lips connect with Helena's, I softly breathe into her waiting soul,

"Helena, by the time I, Darius, your truest dominant, have you pleading with me to let you climax, you will have precariously balanced on the precipice of erotica for the first of many times to come. You will realise that I have now become the man you want to wake up next to every morning, and when that most precious of a thought infiltrates your mind, it will curl around your heartstrings and pluck away at them like a virginal harpist who knows nothing about the instrument that she's nesting between her quivering thighs. You will find yourself readjusting your thoughts accordingly and aligning them with mine. It will be then, without any questions needed, that you will find yourself easily adapting to the single most powerful notion of all and that reflection is that I have now become your hardest goodbye."

'Within Helena's submission, I, Darius, discovered my true dominance.'

~Darius Carter

CHAPTER ONE

The Florist's Boutique

Le souffle du bébé celeste
'Heavenly baby's breath'

LATE SPRING 2014

There are two people you'll meet in your life. One will run a finger down the index of who you are and jump straight to the parts of you that peak their interest. The other will take his or her time reading through every one of your chapters and maybe fold corners of you that inspired those most. You will meet these two people; it is a given. It is the third that you'll never see coming.

That is the one person who not only finishes your sentences but keeps the book.

Author unknown.

HELENA

With a tone of utter amazement, my boss and my closest friend Angelica shrieks out the most piercing of sounds and sings, "It's him, Helena. Honestly, I truly swear to you, that it's most definitely him!"

While the shrillness of the sound of her voice makes me feel as if I have just jumped out of my skin, I shake my head from side-to-side for I am assuming that my *boyfriend-less* friend is off on one of her *I am currently available and I am looking for a partner mission.* Picking up the bouquet of red roses from the countertop, I place the floral arrangement to my nose and deeply inhale the delicate, fresh fragrance that is buried deep within the abundance of soft, dewy petals.

"You *have* to see him," she urges. "For I can guarantee you that when you set your eyes upon him you will most definitely find yourself *swooning*."

"What on earth are you waffling on about, Angelica?" I exclaim. "And would you care to enlighten me as to what you mean by swooning?"

Amused, she gleefully questions, "Yes swooning. I know what it means but do *you* know what it means?"

"Of course I do," I say. "It means to feel, to feel..." I pause, inhale another soupçon of the alluring scent of the flowers and add, "It means to feel, faint."

Clapping her hands together, showing appreciation of my answer, the loudness of her actions making me jump yet again. She then tells me I am correct and replies,

"And by the way, my dearest friend, I'm not jabbering on, but I am telling you, sweetie, that that man sitting across the road in that beautiful, vintage Porsche is most definitely that single, sexy screen god, Darius Carter."

"Well as lovely as that all sounds, I don't think it could be him. It's not possible." *is it?*

I shudder a little at the thought that there could be a slim chance that the mystery man may be him – and that there could also be a chance that *he* may be unattached. Darius Carter has always mesmerized me when I've seen him imaged in issues of celebrity glossy magazines. With him now firmly invading my mind, my fingers trembling slightly, I clumsily secure the green ribbon around the stems, as I go to try to fashion said ribbon into an acceptable looking bow, I hear her quiz,

"Why do you assume such a thing, Helena? Anything's possible in life, don't you think?"

Now feeling a tad curious at who this man may be, I shrug my shoulders, and reply,

"I don't know. It just *can't*."

"Well if you don't know then come and take a look and then you *will* know." She coerces.

I sigh, give in to her ask and swing around. While she waves a hand in the air, beckoning me forth, she hastens, "Quick, quick… Hurry before he decides to buckle up and drive off into the distance."

On reaching the window seat, I plop myself down next to her, place the bouquet on the sill and gaze out of the window. When I see the mystery man run his hand through his mass of dark curls, by that gesture alone of his, my curiosity arises. I promptly arrive at the conclusion that a little spying on this man won't do any harm, would it? So with my interest now stirred, I give in to this ridiculous scenario, playfully jab Angelica on the arm and say, "I'm going outside to sneak a closer peak. You are coming too?"

She jibes me back and giggles, "Of course I'm coming! You know how the old saying, Helena - Safety in numbers?"

"Yes, I do." I laugh, "but I also know the other old saying that two's-company and threes-a-crowd!"

Grabbing my hand, she titters, "*Touché,* Mademoiselle Helena." Giving my palm a light squeeze, she rises to her feet, pulls me up and in a hushed whisper of a voice, as if she is guarding the holiest of secrets, quietly says, "Now I suggest that we stop wasting valuable time, go outside and begin our undercover mission!"

We're both now tittering like a pair of naughty schoolgirls who have decided that to play truant would be much more fun than taking dreary, educational lessons, so as we step out onto the pavement, our childlike moment is interrupted by the shrill sound of the shop phone casting its urgent ring. Releasing hands, I turn to face her and suggest, "I think you'd better answer it, Angelica. It's most likely our latest, overbearing bride-to-be, Ms Prim-and-proper!" I roll my eyes and pull a grimace. She mirrors me and we laugh again. Continuing, I say, "I bet Ms PP is panicking about her flower order again because the last time we spoke, she demanded that the next time she calls she wishes to speak to the boss, and since said boss is you, my dear friend, she's all yours!"

Flaying her arms in the air, she wails, "Why oh why do I have to be the boss right at this particular moment in time, Helena?" she pitifully cries. "I so want to be you – the lowly paid understudy!"

I stifle a giggle at her drama-queen like performance, shrug my shoulders, and then sympathise with her that it's such a shame that she is the boss. She then, with a hint of amusing annoyance upon her face, turns, and reluctantly marches back inside the shop. Now all alone, I look over towards said car and when I see the door open, and a pair of well-attired, long legs gracefully rotate out, for some reason, I find myself pointing my lashes down, only to quickly flick them open to finally see the mystery man in his entirety. *It would appear that Angelica was correct in her assumption of who this man may be, for the aforementioned man is indeed Darius Carter.* He is now casually lounging up against the side of his car and I have become even more curiously intrigued by him.

Trying to remain inconspicuous, I busy myself among the foliage and floras that Mother Nature's beauty has provided, and as I come to the end of my make-believe-fumbling-flower arranging, I clap my hands to signal that I am satisfied with my work. Next, I don't know what made me do this, but I span around on my ballet-pumps, stilled and then focused directly upon him. *It appears that he too is carefully surveying me.* While I held him in my stare, I became aware that my lips were curling up into an 'O' and my thoughts rapidly wandered off as to what it would be like to press my lips up against his and lose myself in a deep, lingering entwining of tongues. With my mind now crammed chock full of silly, girlish romantic thoughts, I broke into one of the sweetest smiles I could muster and tilted my head to one side. As the late spring's breeze wafted through my flowing tresses, I smiled as he slowly removed his sunglasses. *Those dreamy, steely-blue irises of his. A dead give-a-away. Confirmed – it's most definitely Mr Carter.*

While his stare penetrated my very soul, again I averted my gaze down, and turned around. Feeling a little overwhelmed at our silent contact - *This is a form of quantum entanglement, isn't it? – Two atoms colliding and never wishing to separate?* I then, as elegantly as I could manage, walked back into my place of work. *My mission had been accomplished!*

I do believe right before my very eyes, the man of my dreams may, without consciously knowing, have just captured a small fragment of my delicate soul.
- Helena.

CHAPTER TWO

Outside 'Heavenly Baby's Breath'

LATE SPRING 2014
DARIUS CARTER

After applying the handbrake to the latest addition of my ever expanding fleet of cars, I switched off the engine to my silver-grey Porsche 1958 356A Speedster and relaxed back into the seat. Feeling absolutely chuffed to smithereens with my latest choice of vintage extravagance, my frame of mind soon changed to one of a darker, broodier mood when I pushed back the pristine French white cuff that graced my wrist and noted the time on the most favourite of all my timepieces that I owned – A Blancpain Fifty Fathoms watch – it read, eleven-forty-five. Giorgio, my right hand man, had now been gone just a little over twenty minutes, and as I was due to attend a meeting, well more of a tête-à-tête, (one which I must admit to you that I am not looking forward to in the slightest) in just under an hour. I was beginning to turn rather impatient for his return. Now drumming my fingers upon the steering wheel, I narrowed my gaze and spied in the wing mirror. Hoping to see Giorgio striding down the street with my new pinstripe suit, fresh from the bespoke tailors of Saville Row carefully draped over his arm, I was distracted from looking out for him when my vision was drawn to a svelte figurine of a female across the road. She was wearing a rather unflattering, baggy, green tabard over a three-quarter length sleeved polka dot dress, and that ghastly uniform did absolutely nothing to flatter what I assume was an enticing petite figure hidden beneath. While I carefully surveyed her from head-to-toe, she appeared to be fumbling away with an array of flowers, vases and the like on the pavement outside the quaint little florist's shop, which I noted was named *le souffle du bébé celeste.* Being affluent in French, among a few other tongue twisting languages, I translated said shop name as 'heavenly baby's breath'.

"What a charming name." I whispered out. *So pure. So innocent – much like her perhaps? Now wouldn't that just be perfect if she was untouched, untainted by another's hand?*

Now curiously intrigued by this woman, I stepped out of my car, leant back up against it, and crossed my arms. Focusing intently upon *my flower girl,* who was now busying herself among the foliage and floras that Mother Nature's beauty had provided, I don't know why I couldn't help myself from ogling her from the top of her head down to her tippy-toes, but nevertheless I was doing so, and truth be told I was rather enjoying the pleasant distraction from thinking about that damn elusive suit of mine and my forthcoming meeting with my soon-to-be, ex-submissive, *Alice.* On noticing the rich, dark colour of heavenly baby's breath employee's long tresses, I half-smiled, for this radiant beauty was much to my delight, a brunette, and over time, as you get to know me, you will realise that I have always had a secret penchant for hair tones of that particular shade. As she seemingly came to the end of her fumbling-flower arranging, she clapped her hands to signal that she was indeed finally satisfied with her art. I gasped out when I was taken by surprise at her following actions. She span around on her peachy coloured ballet-pumps, stilled and then to my utter and complete amazement she focused directly upon me. Removing my sunglasses, I blinked a few times, adjusted my vision to the soft hues of the

17

daylight, and as she transfixed me within her magnetic stare, I was aware that my jaw had gaped. The reason for this mannerism of mine was because I had just seen her lips curl up into one of the most delectable 'O's' imaginable, and it was then, without any prior warning, my darkest thoughts rose from deep within my soul and I found said thoughts wandering off into the direction of my personal room of pleasure.

Oh what I could do to this woman in the confines of that room. I can assure you that if I was so privileged to have her in situ, I would be feeding that pretty little mouth of hers with more than just an abundance of tongue claiming kisses.

Next, she broke into a very, very sweet smile – *one that was almost too sugary for my tastes but nevertheless, it was an amusing expression, and I was quite looking forward to becoming acquainted with her mouth* – and, as the adrenaline began pouring into my bloodstream, in response to this hormonal onslaught, my heart reciprocated to the adrenal fluid by thumping wildly in my chest. The metronomic beats gained even more rhythm when she tilted her head to one side, and as the late spring's breeze wafted through her free flowing hair, I was mesmerized. She finished me off so to speak when to my complete and utter amazement, she looked down at the cobbles beneath her feet and fixated upon the ground for what seemed to me to be for several minutes. *Per-fec-tion.*

By her, well let's call it *a non-verbal gesture of submission* to me, my manhood made no hesitation into joining into this chance scenario by letting me know it was too indeed aroused by her. While I mentally forced the pleasing sensation in my cock to ebb away, and thankfully said sensation did, I looked up to see that she, my flower girl, had disappeared from my view.

I do believe that the perfect submissive; one than I had been craving for, for so, so long, may have just been birthed right before my very eyes. For me, it was now just a matter of time before she wholly belonged to me.

-Darius

CHAPTER THREE

LA PREMIERE

MID- SUMMER 2016

SUR LE TAPIS ROUGE
On The Red Carpet

DARIUS

Straightening my Armani azure-blue tie for me, Cali, my forever faithful kooky stylist, teeters on her stick thin high heels, places her bejewelled hand upon my right shoulder so she can steady herself, and then looks directly into my eyes. While her green irises sparkle with the usual excitement that fills her on special occasions like these, she pouts her nude, glossed lips at me and asks, "You ready, to step out into the *real* world, Darius and meet your *adoring* public?"

I fake a smile and nod to her a perfunctory yes. Quite frankly I'm not in the least bit interested in *stepping out.* And I know she's well aware of that I am not. She knows that I could do without this tiring extension of being a movie star. Generally I find it laborious having to plaster on a synthetic smile after sitting through the gruelling première of my latest movie 'Balancing on the Precipice of Erotica.' I do so detest watching myself playing back on the silver screen although I must admit, when I heard myself reciting the phrase 'Virginal Harpist', which is written below, in Act four, as it pierced through the silence of the auditorium air, I can honestly say to you that I did crack a wry smile as a cache of hushing whispers rippled through the VIP hand-picked, wide-eyed audience.

"… *By the time I, your truest dominant, have you pleading with me to let you climax, you will have precariously balanced on the precipice of erotica for the first of many times to come. You will realise that I have now become the man you want to wake up next to every morning, and when that most precious of a thought infiltrates your mind, it will curl around your heartstrings and pluck away at them like a virginal harpist who knows nothing about the instrument that she's nesting between her quivering thighs. You will find yourself readjusting your thoughts accordingly and aligning them with mine. It will be then, without any questions needed, that you will find yourself easily adapting to the single most powerful notion of all and that reflection is that I have now become your hardest goodbye.*"

Standing down from me, Cali again asks, "You sure you're ready? You seem to be a little distracted to me."

I dust my latter thoughts from my mind and respond, "I'm fine, Cali. Just stop worrying and tell me when I'm good to go." While she flitters and flutters around me, finalizing my attire, my minds wanders and I start thinking about the impending meet and greet ahead of me. It's so draining and truth-be-told, right now I'd rather be spending the après première relieving my mental and physical stresses within the private confines of my personal room of pleasure. Actually, this instance, I would quite like to see Alice dutifully kneeling before me, whereupon I would be gauging whether she had earned the honour of another one of my sensually arousing floggings.

Maybe after this necessary dutiful task is over, I'll call her up. I know she will most definitely be free. She knows the rules and requirements of our D/arrangement. You see, when I beckon she obediently adheres to rule two and arrives promptly. (Rule one, I'll divulge to you much, much later…) She then assumes a submissive pose of her choosing and patiently waits for my arrival.

Ungratefully, I'm snapped back to reality by the sound of Cali's voice chirping, "Come on, Mr Gorgeous," she teases, "Time to move that pert, sexy butt of yours! After all, can't you hear the desperation and deafening noise of the men and women waiting outside screaming their lungs out for a glimpse of you in the flesh all suited and booted?"

I inwardly groan for yes, I can. *Deep breath – Fake smile – Here goes…*

Putting my best foot forward, I saunter out of the foyer. As my shiny navy blue oxfords grace the blood red coloured carpet beneath my feet, the crowd roars out my name and I look up and… *Bam!* Straight into the brief bursts of the bright lights of the blessed 'Rottweiler paparazzi'! Blinking the blobs of the after-flashes away, as they fade, I start to amble down the walkway, stopping every now and then to strike an alluring pose; one which I know will please my fan's no end.

"Mr Carter, mate!" a voice soused in a thick cockney accent shouts. "So, mate, my mate, you gonna tell us the latest news?"

I'm not your mate! Never will be.

"So, are you going to tell us, the world, if the rumours flying about you and your leading lady are true?"

Bloody hearsays! What is it this time?

"Have you and her been, you know – at it – for the last few months while her rock star husband's been away on tour?"

Muck-stirring weasel, I mutter under my breath. Nosy, conceited bastard! What if we had been 'at it', what was her husband going to do about it? Chastise us with a whip, a crop or a flogger perhaps? Whoopee doo!

After openly laughing out loud at my sub-conscious choice of punishments, I quickly change my expression and now with a deadpan look upon my face, I begin to muse about my leading lady, Suzi. Even though I have to admit she is as hot as hell, from what I've seen of her on the closed set, she's most definitely a natural blonde, and since I don't entertain women of that hair colour, or other men's wives for that matter, my silent answer to him is a firm no. I am not screwing her nor will I ever be doing so in the future!

Passing him by, I flash him a warning glare. He shrugs his shoulders, gives me the middle finger – *how charming!* – and moves on to probe questions at Suzi who is now a few steps behind me and basking in the attention that she so craves. I automatically sign a few programmes and with the end of the path now in sight, an intense sense of relief washes over me.

Keep going Darius. You're nearly at the summit and then when you are free you can text Alice. Just think, when you get back to your penthouse, she'll be waiting for you in your personal room of pleasure – naked – kneeling – hands behind back and her doe brown eyes focusing upon the marble floor that has been chilling her knees for the last hour.

Handing back the glossy mag to a teenage girl, I strut down the remaining line and without any forewarning, my world exploded or imploded – which one I'm not particularly sure, but whichever one it was, my heart was now racing fast and cascading speedily into an irregular rhythm. The only way I can describe the sensation to you is with these following words; *I feel as if an arrow has just been projected right into my very soul and it's lingering in-between my heartstrings for a little too longer than I would expect.* The reason for this untimely experience is...

…There *she* is standing right before me. There is my *flower girl* from just over two years previous standing at the apex of the line.

As I strode in the direction of my flower girl, en route, I extracted my phone from the inside of my jacket pocket, and rapidly texted Cali, instructing her to locate me three red roses. I urged in capitals the exact message that I required to be scribed on the tag. She deftly texted me back with the words, *yes, Sir,* which was followed by a cheeky smiley emoticon blowing a kiss! – gotta love her! I grinned widely because I knew that she would already have them on courier route and I will have said flowers within the next twenty minutes or hopefully a little earlier.

Now with my attention fully focused upon my *flower girl* and with a conscious decision made not to sign any more programmes, I averted my attention away from the world around me and presented myself directly in front of her. Lolling my head to one side, I broke into one of the most enchanting grins I could muster, and while I gave her a sassy wink, my spine stiffened on seeing her cheeks flush – *very arousing*, and she in response to my lash bat, quickly bowed her head. *The dipping of lashes – how unexpected but duly noted.* Next, I put on the sexiest honeyed-tone of a voice I could, and breathed to her 'hello'. On hearing me, I truly hope she did, she slowly raised those alluring long dark lashes of hers for me, and our eyes finally met. With one hand gripped onto the barrier, I extended my other hand to her, and while her eyes widened, drawing me deeper in to her charming aura, I carefully extracted the glossy programme from between her trembling fingers. *Her lips slightly parted.* Focusing directly upon her, I could tell by the glowing of her cheeks alone that she was too magnetically drawn towards me, and while I penned away upon the shiny surface of said programme, I teased her a little by mouthing to her that I'd quite like to take her home and make her skin blush even further. *I wonder if she got that!* Maybe she did for she transfixed upon me for what seemed like minutes, and as I handed her back her paper, she accepted it with a slight snatch. Moving away from her, I waved to her (reluctantly) and the over-excited crowd a goodbye. All I could do now was hope that she would read the scribbles that I had left strewn across the paper:

DINNER 8.30 SHARP ~ HOTEL FLORENCE ~
PENTHOUSE ~ MY DRIVER WILL ASSIST YOU ON THE
BEGINNINGS OF YOUR JOURNEY.
DC

I am now at the end of the line, and two burly security guards have placed themselves on either side of me. While they usher me through into the open air VIP foyer which contains a smattering of early arrival guests, I seize a glass of Perrier water from a passing waiter's tray, toss it back and slam the empty vessel back down onto said tray.

On hearing the sound of glass reverberating against silver, the waiter's eyebrows shoot up and I hear Cali whisper behind me, "You appear to be in a foul mood. What's up with you, Darius?"

Grumbling under my breath, I growl to myself, "Flower girl!"

Cali doesn't hear and I'm thankful for that because I don't want to discuss my mood any further, so I am relieved when she informs me that my earlier flower request has been organized. "It's all done for you Darius," She offers and then points over to my stationary black limo. "I've left the roses on the front seat." She then tickles me to the bone when she titters and adds, "Good luck, Sir, with your 'flower girl'."

She did hear!

On hearing the word luck combined in the same sentence as my flower girl, I spin around, come face to face with her and abruptly snap. "I don't need such a thing as good fortune."

She crinkles her nose and scowls while sharply retorting, "Don't be such a grump, Darius. It doesn't suit your usual charming personality one iota!"

"I'm sorry, Cali. I truly am." I soften. "I didn't mean to bark at you. I guess I'm just exhausted from this whole day."

Her face softens and she soothes, "No problem. If it's any consolation, I'm feeling dead beat too, but I'm guessing after a few glasses of celebratory bubbly, I'll be charged up to party on."

"I guess you will, my sweetie," I smile. "You go and enjoy the celebrations. I'm going to sneak off for some well needed chill out time."

"What shall I say to your guests?"

"Just say I was called away for a short while and I will be returning shortly."

"And will you? – come back."

"No." I wink.

She doesn't intrude any further. She just gives me a brotherly hug, spins on her heel and totters off in the direction of the bar. I too turn and briskly amble off in the direction of my parked car.

Lounging up against the car door, I angle my binoculars from around my neck and rest them on the bridge of my nose. Adjusting the focus, I study my flower girl carefully and as I see her reading my note, I frown as she clumsily stuffs the programme into her jacket pocket. *Why on earth is she creasing it up?* Suddenly the poor female literally jumps out of her skin because Giorgio has just approached her from behind and tapped her lightly upon her shoulder. *Be gentle with my precious, Giorgio.* She turns to face him and as she does, a warm sensation floods through my veins. Panning in a little closer, I witness him giving her as what I can only describe as a kindly, fatherly smile. *Nice one Giorgio – she needs a little reassurance right now.* Next, he tips his peaked, forage cap to her and I know after that gesture, he will be clearly stating to her the following; 'Good evening, Ms. My name is Giorgio and I am Mr Carter's driver.'

On hearing his introduction, I see her falter a little. Guess I was right. By the weakening of her knees, he must have said exactly what I predicated and while they converse further, I see her sway her left hip, drop her corresponding shoulder and peer around him. *Ah, my clever little angel has spotted me.* What a bright, little fragrant minx of mine. I give her a curt wave and disappear around to the other side of my car. Settling into the driver's seat, I watch them fade. He leads her to the waiting limo. The car door is opened for her and I can't help but beam a grin as I watch her enter. With her now where I wish her to be, I buckle up and turn the ignition key. The smile on my face broadens because I now know as Giorgio motors off, with my precious cargo languishing in the back, she will be reading the following:

Helena, a piece of your heart will always be nesting in mine.

As my foot presses to the gas, I am left wondering if she's thinking,

How does Mr Carter know my name?

I guess it won't be too long now until we both find out the answers.

CHAPTER FOUR

La Premiere

Midsummer 2016

Sur Le Tapis Rouge

On The Red Carpet

HELENA

I lean over the protective barrier that separates the general public from the trail of actors and actresses weaving their way down the red carpet and stick out my glossy copy of the premiere programme as far as I possibly can in the hope of catching the leading man's attention. I, along with the other hysterical fans, wave it around in the air like it is a celebratory jubilee flag. He, Darius Carter, is now sauntering his way down the pathway and heading in my direction. I'm desperately hoping that he will notice plain little me at random and choose to sign my programme. *My thoughts often wander back to the spring of 2014 when I first saw him in the flesh and I wonder if at all he... Well... if he noticed me. Probably not.* You see, all I've ever desired, apart from seeing him again in the flesh is to also see his signature stained in ink upon my programme. I stare intently at him, and as he is becoming closer to me, I can now easily study his gorgeous features. Greedily drinking in every square centimetre of his chiselled cheekbones, his ski slope of a nose and the mop of dark silky curls that tumble over his forehead, my tummy flips when he momentarily flicks his tongue over his lower lip. This man is definitely even more captivating in the flesh than on the silver screen. While he continues ambling his way down the screaming line of puppy-eyed, love-sick women (and men), I feel a pang of jealousy hit me deep in the gut for he has just signed a teenage girl's copy, and the way in which she is looking adoringly at him makes me feel dreadfully green with rotten, gut churning envy. *At this particular moment in time, I truly wish I was her instead of me.* As he averts his attention from her to me, he tilts his head to one side and breaks into one of the most desirable grins I have ever come across. Next, I shudder as he sassily winks at me, *yes me* - and by that slow lash bat of his alone, I can't help but feel as if I am starting to liquefy inside.

I bow my head, to stop myself from being on the end of another possible lash bat, but as I do, a deep, honeyed-tone of a male's voice jolts me back into this insane reality. I raise my lashes, and when I meet the owner of said voice, I couldn't halt myself from blushing. Darius Carter - the man I have just sat watching on the open-air screen act for the last two and a half hours is standing tall before me. As he leans over the barrier, he carefully extracts the programme from between my fingers; *I am enchanted by his heart-melting smile.* While we focus upon each other, holding each other within… within our souls, I am drawn to his sculptured lips, and as they move, forming sensual curves and alluring shapes, I can't hear a single word that he is projecting – *Right now, I really wish I knew how to lip read.* The overpowering noise of the screaming crowd has become phenomenal, and it is drowning out each one of his following precious words that I see his mouth trying to convey to me. I am offered back my paper and as a wave of frustration washes over me, I snatch said paper from between his fingers. He then quite simply turns on his heel and casually continues to move on down the row. I frown and curse under my breath at the people around me. If only they had toned their noise down, I might have actually *caught* a few of his words. I go to drop the programme to the floor. *What's the point of keeping an unsigned one?* But as I go to release it from my fingers, something prevents me from doing so. I briefly glance at it and my heart goes into an irregular rhythm when I read the black scribbles strewn across the paper:

DINNER 8.30 SHARP ~HOTEL FLORENCE~
PENTHOUSE ~ MY DRIVER WILL ASSIST YOU ON THE
BEGINNINGS OF YOUR JOURNEY.
DC

The adrenaline is now coursing into my bloodstream at an uncontrollable rate and my mouth is rapidly dehydrating. As my hands begin to tremor, I clumsily stuff the programme into my jacket pocket, and as I feel a light tap upon my shoulder, I quickly gather myself, spin around to see a rather dashing middle-aged gentleman dressed in a smart, black suit standing before me. He gives me what I can only describe as a kindly, fatherly smile. Tipping his peaked, forage cap to me, he then – in such a matter-of-fact tone – clearly states, "Good evening, Ms. My name is Giorgio and I am Mr Carter's driver."

My knees now weakening, I gaze into his eyes which are exuding a gentle softness and somehow I manage to find my voice. It waivers a little and a hello squeaks from the back of my throat. Smiling away at me, he continues, "I would like to say that's it's a pleasure to meet you, Ms, and since you may be dining with Mr Carter this evening, if you do decide to accept his kind invitation, he then wishes for me to escort you to his one of his temporary residences based here in London."

My jaw drops and he continues, - *temporary residence? – how many homes does this man have?* "But first on the way, he has suggested that we should stop off at a boutique of his choosing and purchase you a suitable dress for the occasion."

Still in shock from reading Darius Carter's scribbles, - actually disbelief at what is unfolding before my very eyes - I can't utter a single word in response to Mr. Giorgio, so instead, I croon my neck, peer around him and my vision instantly homes in on Mr Carter across the way. He is leaning up against a black, sleek sports car and he has the most alluring and beguiling look upon his face. He gives me a curt little wave and immediately disappears around the other side of the car.

Now completely dizzy, I look back at the man in front of me, and stutter, "But... But... I... I..."

Giorgio offers his hand to me and for some reason, unbeknown to me, I don't hesitate in settling my palm into his. With his other hand, he gives me a light reassuring pat upon my shoulder. "Come, Ms." He gently urges. "Mr Carter is so looking forwards to meeting you. He asked me to tell you that it will be an honour for him to have dinner with you, and if I may say so, what could possibly be nicer that an evening of light conversation and fine dining with a man of his grace?"

My mind now in a total whirl, I can't respond to him, so I give up on questioning the whys and wherefores of this most craziest of situations. By squeezing his hand, I have silently agreed to accept the invitation and I let him lead me towards the waiting limo. The door is opened for me and I am ushered inside. Seating myself down, I turn to one side, searching for the clasp to secure my seatbelt. As I do, I feel something being placed into my lap. Securing myself in, I glance down to see three red roses tied with luxurious green ribbon. Attached is a small white envelope. My hands now tremoring like never before, I shakily extract the card from its host and my heart almost misses a beat when I read the handwritten inscription:

Helena, a piece of your heart will always be nesting in mine.

As the car motors off, I sink back into the sumptuous soft, grey leather seating, close my eyes and try to make sense of this most peculiar of situations.

CHAPTER FIVE

La Boutique

DARIUS

Grasping the curtain in my fist, I yanked it back, and as it whooshed along the rail, I saw Helena respond to the stark noise by rising onto her tippy-toes. She was reflected within the ornate full length mirror that graces the dressing room of this favourite bijou boutique of mine, and as I dreamily gazed at her bare back, imagining running my tongue down the curvature of her spine, intermittently pausing along each vertebrae to take a nip of her flesh, I felt an all too familiar arousing stir within my groin.

  – Much, much more self-control is required here, Darius – focus.

She pursed her lips, *Oh that delectable mouth* of *hers* and continued to stare into the mirror back at me, and somehow I felt as if she was assessing my image too. I was taken by surprise when she leant forward, pressed her palms flush to the sides of the mirror and held onto it tight. While she remained like this for a few moments, and I believe she was seemingly trying to compose herself, I conjured up my next move. Using her unsteadiness as an opportunity to get close to her, I made no hesitation in lightly padding towards her as not to startle her any further. On reaching her, I loomed over her, and took a deep inhalation of the scent of her femininity. By her fragrance alone, I was smitten. So intensely attracted to her, I took the lead, and I boldly placed my hands upon her person. *She juddered.* Trailing my warm palms down her arms, as her skin brushed against mine, I felt the goosebumps on her flesh raise. I noticed that the hairs on her forearms erected, and as her entire body reciprocated by swaying on the spot, I soothed her by whispering that nothing untoward was going to happen to her and that everything was going to be just fine. On reaching her white-knuckled hands, I gently curled my fingers around them, and one by one, I slowly prised her fingers away from the sides of the mirror. Drawing back her arms, I released them from my hold and as they flopped to her sides, I then steadied her by snaking one arm around her tiny waist. *She's so petite, so delicate and appears to me to be so very fragile, therefore she must be protected at all costs.*

After this first touch of my persona on hers, she whimpered something incoherent and I responded by reassuringly murmuring into her ear, "Shhh, Helena. Just take a few slow, deep breaths and try to let yourself relax. I'm not going to do anything you don't want me to do. Is that clear?" *Well I wouldn't introduce her to anything sexually fulfilling until she'd wholeheartedly agreed to my binding contract of D/s. Would I?*

She shivered again, nodded in agreement and thankfully for us both, she took my advice. While she took in a few draws of air, I placed my hand on the roundness of her shoulder. Sliding my palms down over her pale décolletage, I halted when my fingers located the black silk ties of the dress that were dangling either side of her partially covered, heaving breasts. She trembled and then made a little *oh* sound because I had just taken another liberty with her and pushed my body firm into the arch of the small of her lower back. *My manhood twitched at being in this close proximity to her. If she was*

34

pinned beneath me, heaven knows how my body would respond. Would I be able to control my desire to devour her swiftly in one foul swoop? Would I be able to maintain the discipline of my dominancy and patiently wait like a wolf in the wings for her to signal to me that she needed, that she was aching for my touch? Would I be able to fight my climax so I could pleasure her first? Would I? Could I?

As she let out a muffled whimper, I tightened my grip around her waist. Forwarding myself into her a tad more, I grasped both ties in my fist and yanked them upwards. When the soft sensual fabric pressed against her nipples, I aroused further because I was transfixed upon those beautiful, tightening buds of hers that were now camouflaged beneath the expensive black satin. Lolling my head upon her shoulder, I darted my vision over her cleavage, and as the fragrance of her once again permeated and invaded my senses, I found myself honestly declaring to her, "You are extremely beautiful, my angel. You must know that you are."

With her cheeks flushing and her lips slightly parting, she blinked at me and I blew a light puff of air upon the side of her neck. Lingering my lips briefly upon her trembling flesh, I murmured, "The rise and fall of your beautiful breasts is a picture to behold."

On hearing my words, she took a double blink and I took things one step further by shamelessly grazing my teeth lightly along her flesh – *She tastes divine.*

With my voice low, in a honeyed tone, I suggested, "Let me tie these flimsy straps around your slender neck, for we need to have a safe, tight knot to prevent your dress from unravelling."

Next, as she so slowly triple blinked, in response to her seductive action, my stomach flipped. *What is the woman doing to me?* I took a breath and continued, "And as you get to know me a little better, over time you will realise that I'm rather fond of all various different kinds of bindings."

I could see by her chest rising and falling that her breathing was increasing – *good, I'm beginning to affect her* – she dipped her head, and a guttural groan escaped from the back of my throat. The reason for this sound of mine because I was imagining her like this - *wrists bound behind her back and her dutifully kneeling before me.*

Tugging at the straps tight, I deftly secured them around her nape, nuzzled my cheek into the crook of her neck and breathed,

"I think you need some shoes to go with that hot dress, don't you?"

'Oh' was all I heard her reply.

Snapping my fingers, I blurted for Alana, the assistant, to bring me a pair of shoes for Helena to try on. A tall blonde quickly appeared by my side and offered me the most stunning pair of black Christian Louboutin heels. Nodding, I accepted them, examined them by fingering the satin ribbon ties whilst openly saying that they were just perfect. I then asked Alana if could she please charge the entire outfit to my account and while she was doing so, because she has been so helpful, I wished for her to choose an outfit for herself. She smiled at my gesture, and I was in no doubt that she would choose the highest priced outfit she could find – *women!* As she trotted off, I took Helena's hands in mine, twirled her around, and before she could consciously think what was happening next, I drew her into my arms and she fell against my chest. – She feels good up against me – possibly too good? The surprise of my actions caused her to take a sharp intake of breath, and while she lingered in my hold I slowly trailed my fingers down the centre of her back.

Mentally charting the typography of her spine, I became so lost within her aura that I found myself murmuring, "You are adorable, Helena. There is something so alluring about you, and something so beguiling that you hold my attention like no other woman has ever done before."

She just kept steadily breathing and I kept on hoping she would soon let me kiss those soft, enticing lips of hers. I nudged her again. Another surprised gasp escaped from her person. As her buttocks momentarily swept across the pelmet of the seating behind her, she dropped backwards, and landed ever so elegantly upon the soft red seating beneath her. Without hesitation, I fast dropped at her feet and looked up at her. *Studying her while she seductively nibbles the corner of her lip, by that action alone of her, I'm fast weakening.* Averting my stare from that innocent or not so innocent lip of hers, I took her left foot in my hand, and gently started to massage her toes, while telling her that she has had pretty, small feet and that I wouldn't mind sucking each one of her pinkies in succession. It was as if she had suddenly woken up form a deep slumber because she expressed more than a whisper-of-breath, she stunned me when she just fell about into a series of girlish giggling and while I must admit, I did secretly revel in hearing her girlish laugh, she surprised me even further by asking me if I would like to do exactly that right now.

Oh yes I would indeed my precious, but I can assure you that if I started, I wouldn't be able to stop at just that sensual action and even though I must admit I was amused by her words, I was now both frowning and openly tut-tutting at her for her forthright words. It's imperative that I must show her that I am in control – always.

She then pursed her lips, and I slipped a shoe onto her right foot. Winding the silk ribbon three times around her ankle, I then fashioned it into a bow at the back. I repeated this action with her other foot, and as I did, I did it a little slower than before. The combination of my light touch and the soft, sensuous fabric that was gracing her person caused a light air to escape from between her lips. *Damn those enticing, kissable lips of hers! Focus upon the events of the forthcoming evening Darius – Dinner first, sexual activities a little later on! Remember?*

Regaining my composure, I then rose to my feet, extended my hand to her and lightly declared, "There, Helena. You look just perfect, and I am so going to enjoy dining with you this evening."

Without faltering, she accepted my hand and, I like a pure gentleman aided her to her feet. While she tottered on the thin, high heels, I pulled her into me, held her maybe a little too tight and soothed, "We are going to be so good together, my angel. I think you understand what I mean, don't you?"

She didn't reply to my question. She just wiggled out of my embrace, looked quizzically at me and questioned me.

"Why are we leaving via the rear entrance of the boutique and not the front, Mr Carter?"

Like a fool, I couldn't help from wildly lunging at her, grasping her hand, and squeezing it extremely tight. While I did, she pulled a painful face, but didn't retract from me – *Relief.*

"The paparazzi, my sweetheart. There will be too many of the damn bastards waiting outside the front of the boutique waiting to see me with someone as beautiful as you."

Silent moments passed and as I began fearing that maybe I'd scared her, the tension soon left me when I felt her squeeze my hand back and smile. So I took the plunge and continued with the following speech;

"And, Helena, would you please stop calling me Mr Carter? I only require to be called Mr Carter or sir when we will be in D/s mode. My name is Darius. And it's very irritating that you see the need to be on a formal term with me, since I am intending to get personal with you this evening."

As we began walking simultaneously, exiting the boutique and entering the narrow alleyway that leads to where the limo is parked, I heard an amusing tone rise within her voice, and I can tell you, I was firmly put back into my place when she retorted, "Oh. You are, are you, Mr Carter? And exactly how do you propose to get personal with me?"

Before I could even process her question, she added,

"And please could you explain what *D/s mode* means? I've never heard of such a strange thing before."

Now feeling triumphant that I had gained her attention to converse with me, and that she was showing a feisty side of her character – which I must admit I am looking forward to tempering in the future – with a firmness in my voice, I really took the bull-by-the-horns and launched, "I'll explain your latter ask over dinner and the rest is quite simple really. I am going to make you climax without entering your body. By the time I have finished teasing you, taunting you, you will be pleading with me to take you to my bed and make love to you over and over again."

On hearing my response, she stopped dead in her tracks, wildly tore her hand away from mine, and turned to face me. In the dim light of the streetlamps, her face was a picture to behold. Her eyes were as wide as could possibly be and the fiery, the *almost* you-have-overstepped-the-mark-Mr Carter, look that was now burning in her chocolate-caramel-coloured-irises, made me want to push her flush up against the alleyway wall, pull her panties to one side (assuming she's wearing any) hitch her legs around my midriff and sink my cock deep into her.

Amazingly I was immediately pulled back to a stark reality when she cursed at me, "You are an extremely arrogant excuse for a man. Do you realise that at all? How dare you speak to me in this manner? Just who on this earth do you think you are?"

I felt as if I had been low blowed punched in the stomach. Now feeling winded, I stiffened, quickly mustered my dignity, placed my hand over my heart, and offered her my heartfelt apologies while explaining to her that I was only jesting – *Even though I wasn't!* and that in future I will be more careful with my choice of words. Offering my hand, she swatted it away and as I resisted the temptation to once again soothe her, she then furiously demanded for me to take her home. Stepping towards her, she took two steps back from me and slouched up against the cold, stone wall behind her. Next, as a look of sadness washed over her beautiful face, I felt another gut wrench twist and turn inside me.

Looking at me pitifully, she softened me, she weakened me by politely asking, "Take me home, Mr Carter." A few moments passed and as I went to place my hand around her neck with the hope of drawing her close to me for an impromptu kiss, she quietly implored. "Please… please don't touch me. Just please will you take me home?"

I narrowed my gaze – *This is not how this adventure is supposed to be evolving – I'm not letting her leave me – ever – I can't let her go.* Within the split of a second, I had her enveloped within my cosseting embrace and thankfully she showed no sign of resisting. I began stroking her soft brunette tresses, and as my guard slipped down another untimely or timely notch, – which one I am not sure of – I shocked myself when in such a sad, child-like voice, I, yes I, Darius the dominant actually pleaded, "Don't leave me, Helena."

"Why?" I heard her sweet voice squeak against my thumping heart.

"Because…" I heaved. "Because, I'm so, so sorry for what I just said to you. It's just that you do something to me that no other woman has ever done. You exude some kind of magnetic charm and at the same time, you… you, unnerve me so terribly." I sighed extremely deeply and then divulged. "You make me want to lose control of self-discipline in matters of a sexual nature. You… You..." I stuttered, "arouse me… Yet at the same time your aura conjures up a vast imagery of delightfully erotic and sinful thoughts, ones that have continually permeated my sub-conscious since… since the first day I saw you. Even though I want to, I can't explain to you these intricate thoughts of mine to you at this particular moment in time. I just hope that one day you will allow me to express them to you in, let's say a… a… physical fashion."

As a unique calmness surrounded us, and while we remained in hold like that for some time, and she didn't query – *the first day since I saw you* – so I found myself quietly mumbling something to her about star-crossed lovers. When we did finally release from each other, I looked admiringly at her, tipped my finger under her chin, angled her face upwards and breathed to her one word, and that word was – Stay?

Without another word spoken, she tightened her grip on mine, and led *me* down the pathway towards the waiting car.

CHAPTER SIX

HELENA

Staring directly ahead, on seeing my reflection in the ornate full-length mirror, I wonder what on earth I am doing here. I feel as if I have been transported into some sort of magical and mystical fairytale, and I have yet to turn the last page to discover the ending of this make-believe story that I have become immersed within. As the curtain to the dressing room whooshes back, by its sheer, stark noise alone, I am instantly snapped from my silly, girlish thoughts and I rise onto my tippy-toes when I see Mr Carter reflected back at me. He's changed his attire and I must say he looks extremely dashing in a casual outfit that consists of navy blue slacks and a crisp, white linen shirt. Focusing upon his chest, I notice that the first four pearl buttons of his shirt are undone, and as a rather inviting patch of dark curly hair is revealed to me, once again, I find myself starting to liquefy inside. Averting my vision to his arms, I see that his cuffs are tightly rolled back, revealing a set of strong, muscular, golden tanned forearms. I wonder what it would be like to be cossetted by those arms while I nuzzle into that taut, manly hairy chest of his. My body now tremoring, and feeling a little queasy, I swallow hard, press my palms flush to the sides of the mirror and grasp onto it tight Remaining like this for a few moments, I try to compose myself until I feel his presence settle behind me. Looming over me, he trails his warm palms down my arms and as the hairs on my flesh erect at his touch, his fresh-minty breath settles upon the side of my neck. On reaching my white-knuckled hands, he gently prises my fingers from the sides of the mirror, draws my arms back a little and releases me from his hold. As they flay and flop to my sides, he steadies me by snaking one arm around my waist. At feeling the first touches of his persona on mine, I whimper out – *What is this strange sensation fluttering inside me I am experiencing? What is this effect that he is having upon me?* And he murmurs into my ear, "Shhh, Helena. Just take a few slow, deep breaths and try to let yourself relax. I'm not going to do anything to you, you don't want me to do. Is that clear?"

My mouth has rapidly dehydrated and I am unable to answer him, so instead, I just nod in… in… well, in agreement I guess. As his other hand comes over my right shoulder, and it slides down over my upper chest only to halt when his fingers locate the black silk ties of the dress that are dangling either side of my now partially covered, breasts. *I shiver.* He's now pressing his torso into me, and I shudder again at feeling a fleet of his manhood nudging into my lower back. Letting out a muffled, feeble gasp as he pushes a little more into me, he grasps both ties in his fist and yanks them upwards. While the soft sensual fabric presses against my nipples, it causes them to respond by stiffening. *Oh no, please not this show of arousal right now… Not at this untimely instance.* As I desperately mentally urge my nipples to soften, he rests his head upon my shoulder, and I stare into the mirror to see him dart his vision over my cleavage. As the hedonistic scent of freshly washed male and pheromones permeate my senses and envelope my being, I feel as if I am either about to do one of two things… lift off or faint.

"You're so aesthetically, pleasing my angel," he softly purrs. "The rise and fall of your beautiful breasts is a picture to behold."

Aesthetically pleasing? I've been called pretty, charming, and beautiful before but never aesthetically pleasing! How very peculiar.

I'm now aching to the heart of my inner core, and with the fragrance of his person infusing my senses, I am fast spiralling into such a confused mix of frustration and excitement. I take a deep breath and it's now taking all my willpower not to turn around and slap him for being so forward.

Grazing his teeth lightly along the side of my neck, he then excites me ever further by stating, "Let me tie these flimsy straps around your slender neck. We need to have a safe, tight knot, and as you get to know me a little better, over time you will realise that I'm rather fond of various kinds of bindings."

Why I am doing as he asks? I have no idea. I bow my head a little and a guttural groan escapes from the back of his throat. I wonder why he made that sound at this particular moment in time. My mind is now in a dizzy spin, and I am fast becoming powerless to resist his charms. Tugging at the straps tight, he deftly secures them around my nape, nuzzles his cheek into the crook of my neck and whispers, "I think you need some shoes to go with that hot dress."

Snapping his fingers, he blurts for the assistant to bring him a pair of shoes. A tall blonde quickly appears by his side and offers him the most stunning pair of black Christian Louboutin heels I have ever seen.

How on earth am I going to balance on those spikes without falling flat on my face?

Taking them from her, he examines them by fingering the satin ribbon ties whilst mumbling that they are just perfect. He then adds could she please put my discarded clothes into a bag, ask Giorgio to collect them, and after she has done so, to charge the entire outfit that I am wearing to his account. He then suggests before she tots up the bill, because she has been so helpful, he wishes for her to choose an outfit for herself. *How extremely generous of him, lucky her!* Grasping me by the hand, he swirls me around, and before I can blink, he draws me into his arms. The surprise of his actions causes me to take a sharp intake of breath. Slowly trailing his fingers down the centre of my bare back, the connection of his skin upon mine leaves me completely breathless.

"You are adorable, Helena," he softly murmurs. "There is something so alluring about you, something so beguiling that you hold my attention like no other woman has ever done before."

Now that's better alluring and beguiling. A Much softer, much warmer descriptive word that aesthetically pleasing!

He's now nudging me, and as my buttocks momentarily sweep across something firm, I fall backwards, and I land upon a soft seat. Crouching at my feet, he looks up at me and smiles. Taking my left foot in his hand, he gently starts to massage my toes and tells me that I have pretty, small feet and that he wouldn't mind sucking each one of my pinkies in succession. I openly allow myself to giggle at the mere thought of it, and I ask him if he would like to do just that right now. Frowning and tut-tutting me, he slips a shoe onto my right foot. I am now in awe at watching him expertly wind the silk ribbon three times around my ankle and fashion it into a bow at the back. When he repeats this action with my other foot, he does it slower than before and the combination of his light touch and the soft, sensuous fabric that is now gracing my person is causing me to feel extremely light-headed. A light air escapes from between my lips; he gazes up at me and shoots me such a sexy wink that the air that is still passing over my lips is now followed by my subconscious slowly whispering the syllables of his name.

I think he's heard me express his name. I hope he has.

He rises, extends his hand to me and declares, "There, Helena. You look just perfect, and I am going to enjoy dining with you this evening."

Placing my palm in his, he, like a pure gentleman aids me to my feet. While I teeter a little on the thin, high heels, he pulls me into him and soothes, "We are going to be so good together, my angel. I think you understand what I mean, don't you?"

I can't answer that question at this particular moment in time so I ask him why we are leaving via the rear entrance of the boutique and not the front. He squeezes my hand tight and replies, "Paparazzi, sweetheart! Too many of the damn bastards waiting outside to catch me with you. And, Helena, would you please stop calling me Mr Carter. My name is Darius. It's very irritating since I am going to get personal with you this evening."

As we began walking simultaneously, entering the narrow alleyway that leads to where the limo is parked, I retorted,

"Oh… And how do you propose to do that? And when you've finished explaining that to me could you please explain what D/s mode means? I've never heard of such a thing before."

A chuckle escapes from his lips and he says, "It's quite simple really. I am going to make you climax without entering your body. By the time I have finished teasing you, taunting you, you will be pleading with me to take you to my bed."

On hearing the bluntness of his words, I stopped dead in my tracks, whisked my hand away from his, and leant up against the wall. "You are an arrogant excuse of a man. How dare you speak to me in this manner? Just who on earth do you think you are?"

As the colour rapidly drains from his face and an apologetic glaze casts over his stunning, azure-blue irises, he places his hand over his heart, offers me his heartfelt apologies and explains to me that he was only jesting and that in future he will be more careful with his choice of words.

Offering me his hand, I swat it away. "Please… please don't touch me. Just please will you take me home?"

He narrows his gaze, and within the split of a second, I find myself enveloped within his cosseting embrace. Stroking my hair, he, in such a sad, child-like voice, pleads, "Don't leave me, Helena. I'm so, so sorry for what I said. It's just that you do something to me that no other woman has ever done. You exude some kind of magnetic charm. You unnerve me. You make me want to lose control of self-discipline in matters of a sexual nature. You… You..." he stutters, and surprises me when he blushes and continues, "arouse me… Yet at the same time your magnetic aura conjures up a vast imagery of erotic and sinful thoughts that continually permeate my mind. I can never explain to you these thoughts, and I just hope that maybe over time, you will allow me to demonstrate them to you."

While his words infiltrate my mind and settle upon my soul, I feel a unique calmness surrounding me, and while we remain in hold like this for some time, I am sure I heard him murmur something about star-crossed lovers. When we do finally release from each other, he tilts his head to one side, looks down upon me, tips his finger under my chin, angles my face upwards and breathes one word. "Stay?"

And that simple four letter word was enough to change the course of my/our future forever.

CHAPTER SEVEN

The Limo

DARIUS

For the first time in my life, I have to admit, I have become utterly and totally smitten by Helena. Since the first day I saw her arranging flowers outside her place of work, I felt the strangest of emotions engulf me. It wasn't just the effect she had on my physical being; it was the constant thoughts of her running through my mind day in day out that sent my mind into a whirl of torrid emotions.

I can hear you questioning; if you felt that strongly about her, Darius, why did you not pursue her?

So here is my answer. I agree, yes, I could've searched for her and if I did, it would've been extremely easy for a man of my means to locate her, but you see, I wanted our meeting to be one of a natural occurrence. I am a great believer in kismet and so as fate has prevailed in this instance, here I am with her, on our way to dinner.

While the limo purrs along its chartered route, I recline back into my seat and transfix upon Helena.

"How long will it be until we reach your home, Darius?" she softly asks.

I glance at my watch, arch an eyebrow and feeling a tad curious as to why she asked me in a murmuring tone, I say, "In about half an hour's time," and add, "Why do you ask? Are you getting bored of my company already?"

She tries to stifle a giggle, and when I hear her gibe that yes she has become very tired of my company, I then surprise us both by suggesting that we could kill some time by sharing a kiss. Her eyes widen at my idea and I then politely ask if I may come and sit next to her. She smiles and tells me that that would be very nice. Seating myself next to her, I then ask if I may kiss her – I never ask. *Hell I'm aching inside to kiss those soft, pink lips of hers. She replies to me yes. At last!*

Tenderly cupping the sides of her elfin like face in my hands, I stare intently into those doe-like eyes of hers and while the scent of her floral perfume invades my senses, all I can manage to do is close my eyes and imagine what it is going to be like when I kiss her. I draw a breath and inhale another soupçon of her feminine fragrance. Dipping my head a little lower, a rogue lock of a curl of mine momentarily sweeps across her cheek and I enlighten as I feel her shiver at the softness of my hair upon her skin. My lips are now so close to hers, that I can feel her breath warming the thin fleshes that coat mine.

"This won't be just any kiss, Helena." I sigh. "When our mouths meet, this will be a joining of our souls."

Pinning her body with mine, she sinks back into the leather seating and I tease her by purring, "I'm going to enjoy tasting the sweetness that exudes from your mouth."

To my astonishment, a luxurious smile lights up her face and while I steady her face in my strong hands, my eyelids delicately flitter and flutter like a butterfly taking its virgin flight. Pressing my mouth to hers, on the timely collision of our lips, the sensuous kiss I bestow upon her and she bestows upon me is so captivating to say the least that my heart begins to gather speed, I can hardly contain the thoughts that are buzzing around in my mind. I desperately want to tell her how

I feel about her. I'm aching to tell her that I've fallen for her, hook, line and sinker. I continue dipping, darting my tongue between her lips and scrolling it around her mouth. After some time of losing ourselves in each other, I have to abruptly draw away because the way she's making me feel, I could just strip her bare and claim her right here and that wouldn't be how things are supposed to evolve between us – *would it?* Shuffling upright, she reaches out for me, but I've already seated myself opposite her. I frown and run my finger along my bottom lip.

"You seem disappointed in our kiss, Darius," she shyly states. "Will... Will... You please at least tell me why?"

I want to tell her why I had to halt our kisses. I want to tell her that if I didn't ease back from her I would have let my soul run free and I would've told her just how much I adore her, crave her and ultimately, how much I... I...

I am jolted back into reality by the shaky tones of her voice filtering through the highly polished air of the car. It's small, weak and tentatively questioning my name "Darius?" She whispers. I raise my palm hoping to divert her from asking further. She then crosses her legs, bows her head, closes her eyes and knots her hands in her lap. I avert my gaze from her – I don't wish to see her in such a forlorn pose, so I in turn press the pad of my digit on the intercom button and with a gruffness falling from my lips, I instruct Giorgio to make haste to the hotel.

The limo gathers speed.

CHAPER EIGHT

HELENA

Finally, as Darius leant forward, he cupped my face in his hands and gently pressed his mouth to mine. Then he, with such a gentleness in his voice murmured against my lips, "We barely know each other, Helena, and yet here we are, our souls already beginning undressing each other."

To which, I found my voice and quietly whispered, "Why do I feel so sure that every fragment that's created my person is about to crash into your being?"

"Because, my angel," he sighs, "Many moons ago, we fell in love with each other without knowing."

Relaxing into this fairytale of stories, I give in to the whys and wherefores of why it has occurred, so I ask, "How long will it be until we reach your home, Darius?"

He glances at his watch, arches an eyebrow and responds, "I'd say about in about half an hour's time. Why do you ask? Are you getting bored of my company already?"

I giggle and say that yes I am very tired of his company and I then surprise us both by suggesting that we could kill some time by sharing a kiss. His eyes widen at my idea and he then politely asks if he may come and sit next to me. I smile and tell him that he can. Seating himself next to me, he then asks if he may kiss me. I grin and tell him that he may. Tenderly cupping the sides of my face in his hands, I stare intently into his eyes, and a somewhat quizzical look glazes over his eyes. While his now-all becoming-timeless scent invades my senses, all I can manage to do is close my eyes and imagine what it is going to be like while he kisses me. Will it be like one of his screen kisses – hot, passionate and lingering, or will it be a real genuine, heart-melting and soul-searching one? His fresh breath tingles upon my lips, and as I inhale another soupçon of his fragrance, he dips his head a little lower. Raising my lashes, I exhale as a rogue lock of a curl momentarily sweeps across my cheek. I'm shaking like a leaf at the anticipation of sharing the forthcoming kiss.

With such gentleness, he draws me in a little closer to him, and as the scent of freshly bathed male invades my senses, my head goes into the dizziest of spins. My heart is thumping with such intensity, that every consecutive beat that pulsates feels as if each one is going to break free and burst through my ribcage. Now faltering, he tightens his embrace around me, and gazes lovingly down upon me. His voice soft and soothing, he calmly assures, "Don't be frightened of me, Helena. I'm not going to kiss you unless you truly wish me to."

"I'm… I'm… not…" I stutter, take a shaky breath and resume; "I'm... I'm… not... unnerved by you, Darius. "I'm… I'm… just... in…"

His hand is now cradling the back of my head, and as I feel his fingers stroking my hair, a small moan escapes from my lips. He knowingly smiles, continues caressing me and I liquefy even further, when I feel the heat of his other hand penetrate through the bare flesh that coats my lower spine. His mouth is now dangerously close to mine and as I whimper out again, he whispers, "You're in what, Helena? Tell me."

My voice high pitched, I squeak, "I'm in awe of you."

His lips are now so close to mine that I can feel his breath warming the thin fleshes that coat mine. His eyes are showing me such a deep intensity of passion and I still wonder if he will be acting out one of his screen kisses on me or if it will be one that comes from directly from the depths of his soul. It is as if he reads my mind when he responds, "This won't be just any kiss, Helena. When our mouths meet, this will be a joining of our souls."

Pinning my body with his so I am now flush to the seat, he stuns me by informing me, "I'm going to enjoy tasting the sweetness of your mouth." A radiant smile lights up his face and while he steadies my face in his strong hands, his eyelids delicately flutter. Pressing his mouth to mine, on the timely collision of our lips, the sensuous kiss he bestows upon me is so captivating that my heart begins to race. I can hardly contain my thoughts. I'm aching to tell him exactly how I feel.

I wish I was… was brave enough to tell him that I've fallen head-over-heels in love with him.

He continues dipping, darting his tongue between my lips and scrolling it around my mouth. After some time of losing ourselves in each other's hungry mouths, he surprises me by backing away from me and I become confused as I see him shake his head from side to side.

Regaining my composure, I reach out for him but he's already seated opposite me with a look of sternness cast upon his face.

"You seem terribly disappointed in our kiss, Darius," I offer. "Will you please at least tell me why?"

He doesn't answer. So I place my hands in my lap and stare at my knotted, trembling hands. On hearing him gruffly ask Giorgio to make haste to the hotel, I glance up to him to see him blankly staring out of the window. *Is he lost in his own little world, I wonder? Or is he deep in thought? Whichever, it would be only a matter of time before I found out the answer to my questions.*

The limo then gathered speed.

CHAPTER NINE

DARIUS

Snaking my hand around Helena's bare waist, I drew her flush into me, and as the warmth of skin-upon-skin sent shivers cascading down my spine, I gently settled my other hand around the back of her head. As I felt the hairs on the nape of my neck erect, I liquefied even further when she so sexily whispered, "Tell me what you are wishing for right now, Darius."

With a certain type of bashful shyness in my voice and without hesitating, I found myself quietly murmuring to her, "I wish that you would hurry up and kiss me."

She knowingly smiled.

I openly blushed.

And as she kissed me so deeply, so passionately, and so very intensely, I immediately forgot the air that I was breathing. The reason for me feeling this way was because you see, Helena was the love that came without warning; she captured my heart before I could even say no.

Darius crosses his knife and fork, takes a sigh and languishes back in his chair. Pushing his empty plate to one side, he takes a deep breath, slowly raises his lashes at me and in a matter-of-fact tone, states, "Helena, after kissing you, tasting you, I, I..." he briefly pauses and then continues, "I desire so much more of you. I'm craving to take your beautiful body and your delicate soul to new heightened places of sexual sensuality."

Startled by his words, I look up from my half-eaten plate of seared scallops, dab the corners of my mouth with my napkin and decide that now is the moment to be brave. Without hesitation, I dive head-first into a series of questions. "Why choose me, Darius? Out of all the women you could have selected to... to... have dinner with," I blush and then finish, "why did you decide upon me?"

An awfully long, strangulated pause follows my first question, and while the moments slowly tick by, I nervously chew on my bottom lip. Picking up my drink, I slowly circle the rim of the glass with my finger. He doesn't take his vision off of me. While he creases a concerned frown, he rises from his seat, pushes it back with such a force that the noise of it screeching against the bare marble floor beneath makes me flinch. Walking around to my side of the table, he takes my flute of champagne from between my fingers, settles it down onto the table and balances himself on the arm of my chair. Tipping his finger under my chin, he gazes into my eyes and offers, "As you so eloquently put it, I carefully choose you" – he pauses, drums his fingers on his chest – and when I hear him state, "because I do believe I can train you to become the most loyal and loving submissive that a dominant could ever hope for," with confusion reigning in my mind over this scenario, those words –*dominant and submissive*- I snatch my glass back from him, sweep it to my lips and drain the entire contents in one swift gulp.

"Whoa, my poppet," he softly scolds. "Please slow down. I don't want you inebriated before we even consider taking the first step on our sexual journey together."

Now enraged by his forthrightness and with my mind trying to decipher exactly what the term dominant means, and more so what it may entail, I slam my glass down in a whirl of a frustrated anger and he, in response to the noise jumps off his perch! Rising from my seat, I strut off in the direction of what I hope to be the exit to the foyer while blurting out a garbled mess of my thoughts. "Is that why you wanted to wine and dine me? So you could use my body for your own selfish, perverse pleasures?"

He angrily stomps after me, and I swear, as he does, I can feel the floor beneath me vibrating. Within a split of a moment he is behind me. He roughly grasps me by my waist, spins me around and by the fiery look in his eyes, I am positive that this man is not acting out one of his dramas. *He is a commotion all of his very own!* Tipping his finger under my chin, he tilts my face upwards so our eyes meet and in a quiet whisper he breathes, "It has become perfectly obvious to me that you know nothing about what a dominant requires, let alone what a submissive may have to offer, so with this in mind, I suggest that we should talk no more about it. Forgive me?"

I am so stunned by this whole situation that I can't reply and as his grip on me tightens, he shoves his body into mine. The sensation of his hard, rippling muscles that plank his torso press into mine coupled with his whispering of seductive and erotic words into my ear is making it so hard for me to gear away from him and I'm wavering because he's now explaining to me that he will do anything to make me stay and that would include him paying me for my services. My eyes widen at the latter statement, and I try so hard to wiggle from his embrace but he's now nipping the side of my neck in a gentle but stimulating fashion which is causing me to feel light-headed.

Finding my voice, I pine, "Please, Darius, let me go. I can't do this with you. I don't want to be here anymore with you and... And, I most certainly don't want a single brass penny of your bribing money."

As an energy quickly charges between us and time is shifted through the air, he reels backwards from me. His shoulders sag and his head, he bows. Quickly apologising to me/to the floor beneath his feet, I sense a deep sense of regret tainted within his voice. He continues by telling me that he will now organise for me to be taken home. On raising his head, I see something so shadowy, so empowering hidden behind his eyes. Something that I know if I stay with him, I *will,* over time fathom out. I wonder could that look possibly be one of shame... Does he feel embarrassed for the way he's just behaved towards me? Is his recent manner just a matter of bravado? Is it a front?

Feeling so drawn to him, I say, "I don't wish to leave... yet."

"You don't?" he half-smiles.

"No."

"But you will leave eventually? You won't stay for the whole night?"

"I'm... I'm... not sure right at this moment. Why don't we wait and see what happens."

He sighs deeply and replies, "Okay but I want you to know this, I'm truly sorry," he mumbles and then apologises again. "I *am* really sorry," he emphasises and resumes, "for *all* my rather rash and stupid comments. Forget about everything I mentioned earlier. It was ungentlemanly of me to express such a wish to a lady of your standing." Extending his hand to me, he then asks, "Would you at least let me show you where you would be staying the length of the night if you forgave me totally?"

Now truly relieved that there will be no more talk of said dominance and submission, or finance for that matter, I sigh out, and as he appears to be relentless in his mission to spend time with me, and I am now deadly curious. I soften a little and come to the conclusion that sneaking a little peek at what he wishes to show me won't do any harm because, after all, I am *not* going to stay – but on the other hand, I am ever so slightly intrigued as to see further into his home… *his world.* I offer him my hand. He takes it and we walk over to the far end of the dining room. In the sweetest of voices, he says, "Come on, I think you are going to like what you see when we reach the top of the stairs."

I let him lead me up the spiral staircase, and without a word uttered, he just every now and then gives my palm a gentle reassuring squeeze. When we do indeed reach the top, he is correct in his assumption that I will be amazed, for I gasp out loud at seeing the view from the balconette. It's positively breath-taking. I can see the twinkling lights of the City of London down below, and as the heavy rain beats down and lashes upon the glass, the glowing bulbs glisten, reminding me of a once past, happy, childhood Christmastime.

"By the sound you just made, Helena, I am assuming that you are impressed with what you can see from here?"

I release my hand from his and turn to face him. "Yes, I do, Darius. It's is absolutely beautiful."

Taking a step towards me, he places his finger to my lips and muses, "Mmm." He pauses and then continues, "It's beautiful and beguiling, just like you."

"Can I ask you a question, Darius?"

"Sure," he chirps. "Fire away."

"How do you know my name?"

His mood instantly quietens.

"Please tell me," I gently urge. "Surely you must see that I need to know how?"

Smiling at me he then breaks into a story of his own; "Once-upon-a-time in a faraway land, it was a cool spring morning of 2014. I was leaning up against my car which happened to be parked opposite a florist's shop. When I saw a beautiful flower princess setting up the outside displays of roses and begonias, I felt as if cupid had fired an arrow straight into my heart. I couldn't avert my gaze from you, Helena." He breathes, taps his heart and in such a delicate whisper of a voice hushes, "You had me right there, that second and I can assure you that you always will."

How romantic of you to say, Darius, but please tell me, how do you know my name?

"And as for me knowing your name… I have my ways and means of finding out any information that relates to you."

Curious I ask, "Would you enlighten me as to how you collate your information?"

"Later… if you stay."

I sigh with a defeat (for now) and then ask, "Why did you give me three red roses? Is it because I work in a florist's shop?"

"That's partially the reason why, I did," he grins.

"What is the rest of the reason then?"

"Another time I will tell you but for now," he chuckles, "would you like to know a little more about yourself?"

I giggle at his daft statement and say, "Maybe later," because I am now so enchanted by his persona. Tentatively leaning in towards me, he skims his lips close to mine. His soft breath brushes lightly against my mouth and my subconscious once again taps away in my mind and he nudges me towards a crucial decision. The words tumble fast from my soul, and as they spill out of my mouth, I divulge to him that I will spend until daybreak with him. His lips are now lingering above mine, and as he breathes to me the meekest of a *thank you* that I have ever heard, he surprises me by not kissing me. Instead he retakes my hand in his and leads me down the hallway. We reach the end; he pushes the door open and I am left breathless by the room that is lain out before my very eyes.

"Helena, this guest room will always be at your disposal." He hesitates and adds, *"Forever"*. I hope you will be comfortable spending time here. I shall now leave you to get acquainted with the surroundings. Feel free to enjoy a bath or just relax with some music. I shall return for you in a while and then we can talk some more. It will be nice to get to know each other properly. Agreed?"

I turn to face him, rise onto my tippy-toes and place my arms around his neck. Stooping low, he wraps his arms around my waist, presses his forehead to mine and as I say, "Agreed." I feel his body heave with what I can only describe as a sense of relief. Peeling my hands from around his neck, he coaxes, "Go, go on inside and spend some time pampering yourself. I'll be back soon for you."

I reluctantly turn around and take a step into the room. As the door gently closes behind me, I see a set of French doors at the far end of the suite. I walk over to them, slide the glass open and step out onto the balcony. It's lightly drizzling and I feel as if I want to stand out in the rain, and be cleansed by the elements whilst revelling in the tickling sensation as the droplets coat my skin. As I do exactly that and the wetness filters through my dress, it chills me and I shiver.

I am so lost within this entire situation that I am only brought back to earth when I hear a rather cross voice infiltrating through the elements. "Helena!" It angrily snaps. "What on earth do you think you are doing? You'll catch your death of cold and thought… the horrific image of you ill upsets me furiously."

I jump out of my skin at hearing the stern tone in his voice and spin around. For some reason unbeknown to me, the look of pure distaste on his face amuses me. He places his hands on his hips and glares at me. "Stop laughing, you silly girl. This isn't funny in the slightest!"

"Oh yes it is," I can't help but laugh. "I mean, Darius, just who the hell do you think you are telling me what I can and cannot do?"

He's now stalking towards me and on reaching me, he slips his hand around the back of my neck, tilts his head to one side and numbs me to my core with the iciest of stares. "Well, Little-Miss-Disobedient," he chastises, "are you going to come in from playing like a spoilt brat in the rain? Or am I going to have to haul you, like a bad girl inside and put you over my knee and spank your bottom?"

In your dreams, Mr Carter!

I don't know what made me do this but nevertheless, I did. Grasping his free hand, I placed it upon my right breast. "Touch me, Darius," I implored. "I want you to feel me."

"Helena, please stop," he groaned. "This is not how it is supposed to be."

My voice alarmed, I sarcastically question. "Then tell me, Oh Great One, how is it supposed to be?"

Ignoring my question, his sexuality overrides his common sense and he starts to fondle my breast through the damp silk. Locating my erect nipple, he pinches it so hard that a wail escapes my lips. Mewling for him to continue, I toss my head back in response to his touch, and I moan out as he presses his body into mine, while mumbling, "What the hell are you doing to me, Helena? You're… You are insatiable to say the least."

I can feel his cock now straining against the fabric of his trousers and I so want to release it from its dark holdings and gently coax it into hardness. Brushing my hand down over his shirt-covered taut belly with the full intention of going lower and unzipping his trousers, I moan out for him. He deftly stops the onslaught on my nipples, swats my hand away from his midriff and implores, "No, Helena, please, please stop what you're doing to me right now?"

"I won't stop because I want *you* to take me right now, Mr Carter. I want you to take me right here in the rain. After all, that is what you want too isn't it? You want to *fuck* me?"

On hearing my blunt words, we both still. He stoops down over me, and states, "You… you had better learn to control that foul mouth of yours because if you continue to use language like that, young lady, I promise you I will have to wash those nasty words away with a bar of carbolic soap!"

I pull away from him, head towards the door and repeat rather too loudly and describe in too sexually explicit a detail what I wish for him to do to me.

As I reach said door, he is upon me in a flash. He grabs me by the waist and spins me around. I lose my footing, and as my balance waivers, my back heads towards the wet floor. Saving me from falling, he catches me in his arms and I am stunned when he with sarcasm dripping in his voice, rasps, "Helena, as you so have so eloquently described, if I *fuck* you right now, the mood I am in, I can assure you that if it was at all physically possible, I would break you in two." His eyes are broody and I shudder when he continues and hisses, "As you appear to be so sexually frustrated, I'm imagining you must be so tight from lack of use. If I do dare to touch you between your thighs right now, I imagine that I will have to work you with one or two of my fingers first before you could easily accept the first thick inch of my throbbing cock."

Do I see red again at his rather explicit words? No. I see a whole rainbow of multi-faceted blood-dripping reds and my hand comes up so fast, it hovers inches from his sculptured cheekbone. He catches me by the wrist and I shudder as he glares down upon me. "I don't do violence, Helena. If you want a man that will enjoy that degrading type of behaviour, then I suggest you should leave right now!"

Hauling me onto my feet, I step back from him and offer, "Do you want to know something, Mr Carter?"

Turning his back to me, he gruffs, "Not particularly." Now striding away from me, I'm irritated by his manner and I shout,

"Well I don't care if you don't because I'm going to tell you anyway." He flays his arms up in the air and I blurt, "Do you know that you're even more gorgeous when you are cross? I am mesmerized by the way your eyes flicker with a sexy, glassy glaze and also you make me want to squeeze my thighs together when you curl lips up at the sides. Both of these attributes make me want not only want to kiss you so hard, they make me crave to straddle you, slide down on what I assume is an *overrated* famous dick of yours and fuck your stupid, self-centred, over pompous, brains out!"

He stops dead in his tracks, spins on his heel, points at me and hollers, "You... You... Helena, are fast becoming an annoying little mare and if I was you I'd choose carefully what spews out of your mouth in future when you are in my company. What's falling out of it is pretty abhorrent to say the least."

Now feeling angered at his reply, I fake a smile, laugh and before my brain can engage my mouth, I hiss, "Get lost, you stuck-up *English toff!* It's my mouth and I will say whatever I wish!"

With his hands placed on his hips, he lets out a loud sigh and says, "Helena, I strongly suggest that in the future, when you are in my presence, that you try at least to choose your words more carefully. If you don't, I promise to you, that I will drag you to the bathroom right this very minute and soap out your filthy mouth until the bitterness, the sourness of the lather causes you to vomit every word of foul language out of your tormented soul!"

I am now at a loss for words and truth-be-told, I can't really see where this conversation is heading, so I think it's time to put an end to this ridiculous spat and to call a truce. As I go to open my mouth to offer an end to this, he places a finger to his lips as to signal my silence. I snap my mouth shut and what he declared next left me in a state of stark, white shock.

"And, I may add, I am not impressed by your sarcasm, so therefore I think you should leave. This was a mistake." He emphasizes. "This situ... We…" – he stutters – "are not going to work. Tapping the face of his watch, he raises his eyebrows at me and then in such a formal tone, states, "I'll have Giorgio ready and waiting for you in exactly one hour. Take a shower if you wish to warm up. If not, then so be it."

Roughly brushing past me, nearly knocking me off balance, he snorts and as I hear the door slam exceptionally hard behind him, I wince at not only the deafening sound of said door but also at the curses of my name as it fades into the distance.

I took a shower, extracted my folded clothes from the boutique's bag, and quickly dressed. Before I left, I hung the dress that Darius had bought for me onto a hanger, placed the heels next to them and left my room. En route through the condo, I never passed him by. Thankfully or not thankfully – which, I'm not sure. For if I had, I may have fallen into his arms and told him exactly how I feel about him and in light of what had recently transpired, that wouldn't have done at all.

CHAPTER TEN

Parting Is Such Sweet Sorrow

Standing in the foyer of the building, I wonder what had just occurred. I mean not just over the last few hours but from the moment I entered into Darius' world. All I want to do now is to be alone in my apartment, take a nice hot bath, sip on a cup of steaming cocoa, snuggle down under the duvet and watch Bridget Jones' Dairy – *for the millionth time*. Stepping out in the evening's damp air, I see Giorgio holding the car door open for me. I gesture to him as if to say I'm fine and I'll make my own way home. He doesn't approach me, he just closes the door, turns and walks back into the building.

Ambling through the emptying streets of London for what seems like an eternity, with my mind in turmoil and my heart now blistering into ragged tatters, I try so hard to hold back my emotions. While I wrestle with my feelings, I find myself ending up outside Baker Street tube station. Shivering a little, I pull the sash of my mackintosh tight around me and while the light misty, summer's rain envelopes me, and the soft warm, wisps of a multide of droplets settle upon my lashes, I take a few blinks to wash them away. I am unsuccessful in my task because nature's wetness is relentless in her onslaught. As my sad, salty tears, amalgamate with the elements, my heart-broken thoughts unashamedly seep from the corner of my eyes and trickle down my cheeks. Wishing I had never had that spat with Darius I increase my pace, only to halt when I reach the top step that leads down into the depths of the London underground. Holding onto the handrail, I take a step down. As a joyous, laughing couple pass me by, I pause, and linger for a while musing as to if I should descend further into the station, forego my cocoa and movie plan, turn around, hail a cab and go back and try to make it up with Darius. *No, go – for I can't even remember where his temporary residence is.*

While my mind fogs and my temples thump, I hear a voice, angry but yet concerned, behind me boom, "Helena, what on earth do you think are you doing? You didn't think for one minute that I was going to let you walk home in the damp, dark of the night, did you? Anything, anything could happen to you!"

Relief floods over me in waves at the sound of his voice.

My voice shaky, I don't turn around and I murmur, "I wasn't going to walk home. I am fully intending to take the tube."

His voice strong and curt, he replies, "No you are not. There is no way you are travelling on public transport in this... this erratic emotional state. If you wish to go back to your home, I will take you. *I* will drive you."

"Well," I pitifully say, "you partially created this *emotional state* that I'm in, so please, please," I weakly implore, "Please leave me alone, Darius."

But he didn't adhere to leaving me alone and I'm secretly pleased that he chose not to.

His arms are now snaking around my waist and I am gently ushered around to face him. Tilting his head to one side, he studies me with such intent and quietly says,

"I don't know what it is about you. You evoke so many different emotions in me. Joy, anger to mention a few. Not only have you captivated me, but you also have this fearfully magnetic pull that I can't manoeuvre away from. I just can't stop thinking about you, Helena."

On seeing the warmth, the compassion within his heavenly blue irises, I go to speak. I so desire to explain to him why I acted as I did. I owe him an explanation as to why I wanted us to be over before we'd even begin, don't I? He draws me into him. I do not resist against him. I don't want to. We must've remained in hold for what seemed like for ever, for when we stepped back from each other, we both looked like a pair of dishevelled, rain-soaked lost puppies!

He half-smiles at me and asks, "Do you want to know something?"

I nod. "Not only are you a stubborn mare but you are also an extremely feisty one, Helena."

I shrug my shoulders and quip, "It does help to have spirit when one is around you."

Rolling his eyes, He runs his fingers through his damp hair, sighs and breathes, "I like those attributes in you. Will you please come back with me? Stay for the night – maybe Saturday into Sunday too?"

That's pushing it a bit far, Darius, the whole of the weekend.

He then rushes into a further mindboggling speech. "I mean, we could start this adventure all over again. We could call this a getting-to-know-each other- date weekend and you can stay in the guest room. I'll take you home Sunday night. And if after, you decide that you don't want to see me again, I'll… I'll..."

"You'll what?"

He drops his lashes, resists a tad, and then softens me when he mumbles, "I'll try very hard to forget you."

Oh please don't forget me, ever.

I extend my arm to him and he places his hand in mine. "I... I ... don't want..."

"You don't what, Helena? You can tell me."

"I don't want you to forget me," I shyly say.

"Then it's quite simple." He sighs. "Then you *must* stay."

"All right," I respond without hesitation. "I'll allow you have the pleasure of my company until Sunday evening but there is one extra special golden rule."

His shoulders slump and he lets out a deep groan. "Enlighten me, as to your *unbreakable* rule, Helena."

"There is to be no more talk about that Dominance and Submission thingy, okay?"

I sense a reluctant – *okay, I promise* – fall from his lips and it is rapidly followed by him expressing, "But do you think you might allow me to kiss you again?"

"Maybe... We'll see."

A brief look of defeat crosses his face only to quickly disappear. "Now that we have that settled, let's go *home* where I will run you a bath, and after you've showered I, your king, will challenge you, Helena, my queen to a game of chess."

King? Queen? Chess – I've never played chess before – is there no end to this man's ideas and talents?

CHAPTER ELEVEN

FRIDAY NIGHT
DARIUS

With one arm, I snake it around Helena's petite waist, and draw her flush to me. As I focus intently upon her alluring, chocolate-caramel, coloured irises, I can detect that her eyes are filled with a thousand quizzical questions, which I am sure of, I will soon be answering each and every one with the sincerest of truths. Slowly, with the other hand, I tentatively grasp a fistful of her auburn hair, and her head angles upwards. While her lips sweep elegantly along mine, she weakens me by so softly breathing "Is this how things are meant to be between us, Darius?" I push my naked body into hers, and as I feel her body warming against mine, I dip my head a little lower, and press my forehead to hers. While my cock twitches against her belly, her question sounding a little more urgent than before, she murmurs into my mouth, "Is this how things are meant to be between us, Darius?"

Truthfully, I can't answer her at present because all I can think about right at this very moment in time, is lifting this angel of mine into my arms, and carrying her towards the safety of my bedroom.

HELENA

After we had both taken a shower (separately, I may add) I towel dried myself, picked out from the vast array of lotions and potions that adorned the shelves of the guest room a white bottle that displayed the Coco Madamoiselle Chanel logo, and applied a lavish amount of the luxurious crème to my entire body. Now feeling sensual, I walked naked out of the en suite and headed into the bedroom. Opening a set of closet doors, which to my utter amazement I found adorned with a selection of rather stunning outfits, which as I flicked through, all appeared to be in my size. Sifting through the rails looking for something suitable to wear and hoping I would come across a pair of jeans and a t-shirt, I was shifted from the latter idea when my fingers brushed against something that was blood red in colour. Taking the garment off the hanger, I held it up against my bare, scented flesh and while I revelled in its heavenly softness sweeping across my skin I decided that I would wear this. The safety of jeans and t-shirt had become no longer an option. I slipped into the gown. As I was tying the sash tight, my vision fell upon a pair of red kitten boudoir heels at the base of the wardrobe. Picking them up – *size four – my size* – Smiling at how Darius must have put himself out to find out not only my correct dress size but shoe size too, and feeling like Cinderella who was about to meet her prince charming, I began imagining Darius making love to me while I was wearing this attire. *If only.* To complete my outfit, earlier I had noted a bottle of Coco Madamoiselle Chanel Parfum on the dresser, so after applying a liberal spritz behind my ears, on my décolletage and on the inners of my wrists, I surveyed my reflection in the mirror. Feeling pleased with the way I appeared, and secretly hoping that Darius would too, I wished myself good luck and promptly left the room. Carefully making my way down the spiral staircase, I headed in the direction of the lounge, and as I walked into the room, I was greeted by the shrillest of wolf whistles cutting through the air.

"You look stunning," the voice complimented. "That sexy shade of red most certainly suits you, Helena."

I politely thanked him and told him that he looks very nice too in just a pair of sweatpants that were hanging off his lean hips. *Why didn't he make an effort too? Well never mind because for I quite like what I see seated before me!* Patting the cushions next to him, he ushered me over to join him. On reaching him, he grasped my hand and yanked me downwards, until I found myself next to him.

Taking me by surprise, he curled one hand around my neck, and drew me into him. Nuzzling his cheek into mine, he whispered, "You smell so divine, Helena. I could make love to you right here, right now."

I wish you would, Darius.

Without releasing me from his hold, while his freshly bathed scent invades my senses sending me giddy, he purred into my ear, "If I did consume you, do you know what would happen to us?"

My head now whirling fast like a child's spinning top toy that has been firmly depressed over and over, "No, I don't," I gasp, "En... en… enlighten me."

"You, my precious, will melt on my tongue." He sensually whispered.

Oh good grief... Is such a sensation possible?

"And you," I so quietly hushed, responded with these words that came from out-of-the-blue, *"will dissolve on mine."*

He drew back from me and while his eyes ignited with a simmering passion, one that I felt any minute now would explode into reality, he broke into a triumphant smile and I wondered if I soon will be indeed *melting-on-his-tongue and he would be dissolving-on-mine.*

His stare is now piercing through my being and I am beginning to openly tremble in anticipation for his next move. *Am I about to be made love to by this man?* I needn't have shaken so openly for he took my hand in his and we both rose to our feet. Leading me across the room to a table situated next to the floor to ceiling window, he drew back a chair and asked me to sit down. I did and he seated himself opposite.

"Before I claim you, Helena, we have a game to play."

Not noticing the game that was laid out on the table that separates us, I quizzed, "What type of game do you have in mind?"

Tapping the table, he asks, "Don't you remember what I told you earlier when we were at the tube station?"

"Erm... Erm...vaguely, I think."

"Well then why don't you take a look what's on the table and then your memory will be refreshed."

I do and the penny soon dropped. *Yes. Chess.*

In a matter-of-fact tone, he then says that even though I am looking very alluring and extremely fuckable, he is going to try very hard not to think about taking me to his bed and that we are now going to play said game of chess... and also that before we begin our game, he has something that he wishes to explain to me. *I am now mute.* He then asks me if I am ready to listen to what he has to say. I quite simply nod in agreement.

"Helena..." he pauses... "If you decide to honour me by allowing me to become your dominant, this is how I see my service to you."

"But... But you promised me you would not mention this subject again," I groaned.

"Some rules are meant to be broken, don't you think?" He coolly replies.

I drop my lashes, blink a few times and stare blankly at the chequered board. "Well maybe, I guess some are."

His voice sounding a tad irritated, he asks, "Well, do you want to hear what I have to say or not?"

I inwardly silence because, yes a part of me wishes to hear what he has to say and I have to admit that now I am here I am extremely curious as to what may spring forth so I tell him to continue.

Leaning forward, he rests his elbows upon the table, half-smiles at me and then resumes. "This is my take on what I see our impending D/s relationship not only to contain, but also what may, over time, blossom from the raw intimacy of this moment."

I gulp!

"I see said relationship as being something far deeper and much more emotionally grounded than simply having kinky sex with you. By the same representation, I cannot say that I would align it to ever being positioned upon the plain of a spiritual experience, although I must admit it is possible there are some deep emotions hidden within that most mystical of levels, and who knows, maybe one day they can, possibly, without one knowing, become entwined within the tangled web that we are about to weave. On balance, for me, D/s is a plateau for relating deeply with you in a manner in which we both must be comfortable with. We must make it satisfactory in all manner of ways."

My mind is now in a swirl at his words and as I find myself and to ask him what I consider to be a very important question. He raises his hand as if to signal my silence. I quickly snap my mouth shut. I am now in complete awe of his declaration that I decide for the moment not to add to his words, as he changes tack and gaily enquires, "Have you ever played chess before?"

I pick a canapé from the plate nearby, pop it in my mouth and shake my head as to signal a no.

A sexy smirk crosses his bowed lips and as they curl up at the corners, he chuckles, "Oh well, never mind. I'm sure a woman as beautiful and intelligent as you will turn out to be a worthy opponent in a multitude of different arousing areas!"

I swallow my mouthful with a nervous gulp and inform him that I don't really understand what he means. He seats himself, stares at me hard and tells me that by the time dawn breaks tomorrow, I will have full knowledge of exactly what he means. Changing the subject, he then instructs, "You're going to be the white marble pieces, because I think the virginal colour suits your somewhat innocent personality."

I burst out laughing and I can't help myself from quipping that the colour black would suit him very well because, to me, he appears to be a very dark and mysterious man. He doesn't take his vision off me. The way he's narrowing his eyes while seductively chewing the corner of his lip is doing more than sending a series of ice-cold chills surging down my spine – it's positively engulfing me with an almost raging, burning desire to swipe the chessboard to one side, crawl onto the table, place my hands on his bare biceps, grip him firm and yank him hard in my direction until we are so close that we are at loggerheads.

Cocking an eyebrow at me, he smirks and then chirpily enquires, "So, Helena, are you going to make your move yet? I wish you would because by the way you are fingering with that poor little pawn, I think you ought to."

"Why?" I titter.

"Well, my sweetheart, it's because from where I am sitting, he appears to be getting damp between your sweaty thumb and forefinger and I fear if you continue fondling him in that enticing manner, he may soon fall from your slippery grasp!"

I astonish at his rather descriptive and suggestive question and he in turn responds by leaning over the table and placing his hand over mine. As he does, the charge of electricity that ignites between us causes me to drop said pawn – and that is when I realised that I didn't stand a chance in either beginning the game, let alone the good fortune of winning.

Moments pass and he then suggests that it would be a nice idea if we retired onto the sofa. We do. Seated opposite each other, he asks me to move close to him, so I do. I want nothing more than to be near to him, to feel his body pressed up against mine. On reaching him, I turned my back to him, reclined and languished back into his bare chest. *I can't believe that I am actually here, draped in his arms.* While he trailed his fingers lightly up and down my forearms, each one of the tickles sent shivers radiating through my entire body.

Feeling the strong, metronomic sound of his heart thumping soundly against my back, I closed my eyes only to flick my lashes open when I heard him sweetly say, "I'm glad you agreed to stay, Helena, and I'm more than happy you are allowing me to touch you."

"On both of those accounts, I must say I agree."

A few silent moment pass by and it is only broken when he surprises me by asking, "Would you like to go out for dinner one day with me?"

He's planning a future for us together? He wishes to be seen out in public with me?

"Yes, that would be really wonderful," I chirpily reply. "If we do go out, would that mean... mean…"

Kissing me on the side of my neck, he asks, "Mean what, my precious. Tell me?"

I feel my face reddening and while he starts tenderly stroking my hair, I say, "Mean that by stepping out together we will be a couple – officially."

A pregnant pause follows and I'm not sure if he is going to respond to my question so I pretend to myself that I never asked. Suddenly I feel the tightening of his thighs around me, and I am held in a vice like grip. In a flash, I am flipped over onto my back. Bearing down upon me, his eyes are sparkling with a sense of mischief and as he entwines both his hands in mine, knotting our fingers together, he pins each arm of mine in turn above my head. I am tremored when he so quietly breathes, "We *will* become a couple when *I* make love to you, alright?"

"Yes." and the reason for my quiet cry was because not only are his lips brushing against mine, but I can also feel his cock straining at the knitted fabric of his sweatpants.

While he presses into my body, he winks at me and said wink is followed by him melting me even further by sexily whispering, "I can tell by the way that your breathing is increasing, you're aching to feel me buried deep inside you aren't you? You want me to kiss you again, don't you? You want me to make slow, sweet love to you right here this very minute, don't you, Helena?"

I give a curt nod because I do so desire all of those three things and with hopefulness in my voice, I stop playing hard to get, give in to his charms and shyly ask, "When will that delightful moment be?"

He chuckles, quickly draws back from me and settles onto his haunches. Without breaking vision with me, as he fumbles into his pocket, I wonder what he's going to produce for within. On seeing him withdraw a gold foil packet, another penny drops! I nervously chew my lip and when he places the shiny square between his teeth and deftly rips it open, I shuffle upright. Now focused intently upon him, as he extracts the content from within, without another word spoken, he then shimmies down the waistband of his attire over his lower body, revealing his nakedness to me. Not only has he gone commando under his sweats, but from what I can see his nether regions are void of any hair. With his glorious manhood now on display to me, it takes no time for my cheeks to turn a deeper shade of blush.

"By the way that your cheeks are heating, Helena," he quietly laughs, "I can tell that you are impressed by what you can see."

I'm more than impressed, I am positively swayed. I can't speak. In fact I don't think I can even move a muscle. I am so gob-smacked by his forthrightness and his manly beauty that I am stunned into a complete silence. Next, he takes my breath away ever further when he slips a hand between his legs, cups his balls in the palm of his hand, and gently plies them whilst repeating his last question to me. *I've now unquestionably evolved into a dizzy mute!* While he continues his erotic tease, I begin to wonder if I will be able to accommodate such a magnificent member as his. As I ponder more sensuous thoughts, he stops teasing himself and with his free hand he offers me the translucent latex. Now staring intently at me, he asks me to position myself up onto my knees. I don't oblige him by taking the condom, because all of a sudden a wave of uncertainty washes over me and I feel unsure about making love with him.

Resting back on my haunches, I look at him and he has a puzzled expression upon his face. Quizzing me he asks, "You seem a tad confused, Helena. Care to share your thoughts with me?"

"I... I..." I stammer, "I'm feeling a little overwhelmed by this moment."

A sympathetic look crosses his face and he sighs, "Oh sweetheart, remember, I've told you before that I wouldn't do anything you didn't want me to." and then he actually makes me relax slightly by naughtily suggesting since his cock is rock hard, maybe I would like to assist him in deflating it!

Clasping my hand over my mouth, I stifle an impending giggle and then reply, "I've... I've never been asked to do that to, with a man before."

His eyebrows shoot up and he exclaims, "Truly, precious, you've never assisted a man inputting on a condom before?"

My cheeks now on fire at the thought of doing such an action, I mumble an embarrassed, quiet no.

"Then answer me this. Have you ever felt a man release his climax in your hand before?"

"No." I squeak.

"Would you like me to be your first?"

"I... I... think so."

"You either know or you don't, Helena." His voice soft and coercing, he asks, "Which is it to be? A simple yes or a positive no will suffice."

Yes, falls without warning from my lips.

In an instructive manner, which leaves no room for debate, he then asks me to grip him firm. My left hand now trembling, I dip it lower, settle it between his strong thighs and as I do, caressing him for the very first time in the bare flesh, I openly tell him that he is beautiful. He smiles and wistfully tells me that he knows how desirable he is and that I am a very lucky lady to be here in his presence. *Arrogant man you say? No, to me, he's just an extremely confident and alluring specimen of a man.*

With his cock now encircled within my palm, the warmth of his flesh coupled with the ever-increasing firmness of his muscle, which is becoming stiffer by the moment, I am left feeling giddy. Placing his hand over mine, he coaxes me to move my hand up and down his shaft until I feel him throb to a peak of erectness. Flinging his head backward, as a low-grating rumble rises from the back of his throat and he hisses out through his clenched teeth. Grasping my free hand, he places the condom into my palm and curls his fingers around, moaning, "I want to be inside you, Helena. I'm aching to feel your soft, moist folds clenched around me."

I am now feeling so sexually charged by this entire experience and as my confidence seemingly returns, I close my eyes. He then directs, "Pinch the end between your thumb and forefinger, then place the rim over the crown of my cock and slowly roll it down to the base for me, Helena."

Momentarily pausing, he shakes his head from side-to-side and laughs, "I know exactly what you're thinking!"

"Really? Then tell me o-confident one," I jest, "What am I thinking?"

He snorts and then replies, "You, you little minx are thinking that this rubbery friend of ours isn't going to be stretchy enough to cover the entire length of my cock, aren't you?"

He's quite right in his assumption.

With my heart now racing fast, I don't answer him, instead I swallow hard and I can't resist teasing, "What will you do if I don't put it on for you?"

Narrowing his gaze, he muses and surprises me when he replies, "That's simple. I'm not going to claim you unless I am wearing it."

"Why?"

"Carless mistakes can make unplanned and sometimes unwanted babies, Helena."

"You don't want to become a father?"

"Well not just yet, my precious." He sighs. "I'd rather practise with you for a while."

"I guess practise makes perfect." I tease.

He nervously laughs and as I understand him entirely, I say, "Maybe I don't want the offensive, unfeeling sheath inside me."

Between us.

Now squinting at me, he shrugs his shoulders, and I'm caught off guard a little when he gruffs. "Well it's either that, precious or because now that I am fit to burst, if you don't wish to oblige, I guess I'll just have to nip off for a wee while and take pleasure in pleasuring myself."

Jerking back from me, his blood-gorged pole of muscle springs from my hold, and he adds, "If you won't aid me then I can assure you, Helena, that I will slope off to my bedroom and leave you alone."

I too raise my shoulders to signal to him. *I couldn't-care-less if you did slant off to your boudoir and hand-fuck yourself!* Only to stifle another giggle when he with a soupcon of jesting in his voice, continues, "And by the way I want you to know that I'm excellent at hand-fucking my cock!"

Touché!

Coming closer to me, he tips his finger under my chin, angles my face upwards and asks me concentrate upon him. While I stare intently at him, he takes the condom from between my fingers, dangles it in front of my face and states, "Well since we are not going to be using this little fella, I guess I am going to redress myself."

Flinging the rubber to the floor, he springs to his feet, yanks up his sweats, adjusts himself as best as he can and queries, "Why are you so anti-condom?"

Taking a deep breath, I admit that there is no need for him to have to use a sheath, for I am on the contraceptive pill. On hearing my words, a look of despair broadens across his face and he snaps, "You're what?"

I coolly repeat that I am on the contraceptive pill and have been for the last year. I hear him mumble *Oh fuck it!* And I frown as I watch him angrily stomp off in the direction of the drinks bar.

"What's the matter?" I shout. "Are you having a hissy fit because you can't get your own way?"

As my words filter through the air and penetrate his mind, he stops dead in his tracks, shoves his hands in his sweat pockets and slowly twizzles around to face me. The dark, brooding glare in his usually sparking azure-blue irises is enough to make me shudder and wonder what's about to happen next. With a challenging tone in his voice, he sharply rasps, "Hush that mouth of yours, Helena!"

Here we go again!

"What will you do if I don't quieten?" I query.

He doesn't reply, he just turns, swipes a bottle of Glenmorangie scotch from the bar surface, locates a tumbler, unscrews the cap, and then pours a generous measure. Tossing it back, he slams the glass down, and spins around. Languishing against the rim of the bar, he raises his arms, and places his hands on the back of his head. While his body stretches, and I see every finely tuned muscle that graces his planked midriff flex, I feel a deep tingle, flutter between my legs.

What would it feel like to have his tight, hard muscles pressing against my naked breasts, I wonder?

I am snapped from my thoughts when he rests his hands on his hips and begins to set out a series of probing, barraging questions. His words now riling me, I jump to my feet, and holler,

"It's none of those things, you man. Anyway," I sourly add. "It's none of your damn business you nosey parker!"

I think I've irritated him too for he's now striding towards me, and his nostrils are wildly flaring. As he comes closer, I swear I can his irises flickering with anger and sparking with a green, envious jealousy. On reaching me, he lunges at me knocking me off balance, and I fall back onto the sofa.

I'm left crazed and confused when in a flash, he covers my body with his and rasps, "It *is* my business." He firmly states and then emphasises. "Everything you do while you're with me is of my concern. So, if I was you, precious, I'd answer my questions promptly."

Turning my head to the left so I don't have to look him directly in the eyes, I sarcastically reply. "Fuck off, Carter! And for goodness sake, will you please stop calling me precious. I'm not a rare jewel."

"Tell me to fuck off again, Helena, and trust me when I say, I will hoist you up, place you over my lap and spank you until you whimper out to me an apology. And double trust me," he sternly affirms, "When I say this; there will be *no* limits to your punishment."

I am now so enraged by his manner that once again that foul word spews from my mouth. He reaches for my face, holds me in his grip and I close my lashes. I try to avert him but he has me. While his lips move over my throat, up my neck and press against my mouth, he insists that I open my eyes. By the angry tone of his voice, something defensive inside me fuels and with all my might, I place my hands over his heaving pectorals and with all my bodily power, I shove him back. As I roll out from underneath him, I plop onto the floor with a thud straight onto my buttocks. "Ow! Ow! Ow!" I wail, roll over and place my hands on my behind. "Ouch, that really hurt my bottom."

Crouching down beside me, he hisses, "When I catch you, Helena, you will know exactly how a smarting bottom truly feels."

Before he can touch me, I have already sprung to my feet and I am off. With my bottom cheeks numbing, I scamper quickly in the direction of the stairwell. On reaching the top, I hear his footsteps thundering and his voice boom through the air. "Don't be afraid of me, Helena. I'm a pussycat really!"

Yeah right! You seem to be more like a testosterone pumped, rampant, stalking panther to me at the moment!

Without turning around, I hurry down the corridor and holler,

"I'm not scared of you, Darius."

Finally reaching *my room,* I bolt inside and go in search of my bag, only to freeze when I hear him state,

"If I was you, Helena, I wouldn't even dare to consider leaving me." And I root to the spot when he finishes his sentence by claiming, "You belong to me and you always will."

Such boldness, Darius or perhaps maybe arrogance?

Glancing up to see him standing in the doorway, I inwardly groan at seeing his sweatpants slung way too low off his hips. Trying to remain focused on my task in hand, as I note that the bulge in his groin has shown little sign of softening, my mind wanders to a rather erotic thought. Now wholly transfixed upon him, I have visions of me sinking to my knees, freeing his cock from its dark confines and pleasuring him with my mouth, my tongue and my hands. He's now temptingly running his fingers through his silken, dark curls, and I have to ask myself – *Even when he's cross, why does he have to always look so damn sexy?*

Finding a voice, I retort, "No, I am not yours. I belong to no one except myself. And... and," I add, "If I wish to *leave you*, I will!"

He's now boldly striding towards me. I try ignoring his presence, and I carry on stuffing my clothes into my bag. On reaching me, he snatches the holdall from me, tosses it to the floor and grabs hold of the neck ties of my dress. Looming over me, he yanks me into him, bears down upon me and in a authoritative tone, growls, "You *are* mine, sweetheart and don't you ever forget it."

I bravely mouth to him another obscenity. I just couldn't help it. And for that display of foul speech, in a trite, he took a step back from me, paused and then roughly tore the dress from my upper body. Glaring at me hard, while I discarded said dress, he narrowed his gaze, frowned and then deeply sighed, "You're a feisty little mare and you need to be not only broken in hard, but you also need to be trussed up and tamed."

For his outright arrogance *that foul word*, once again rose from my mouth!

"This is your last warning, Helena. If you say that to me again, I can assure you that you are going to be in a whole lot of trouble."

For some reason I began to find this whole ridiculous event funny and through my giggles, I sniggered, "Oh really, Darius. Am I?"

"Yes," he gruffed, "You most certainly are."

On hearing his reply, I antagonised, "Well then I guess to prevent me from being a naughty little girl you are going to do exactly what you previously stated and go ahead and to try and tame me!"

While he beared down upon me, my spine stiffened and as he answered, "I will soon have you docile," I raised both my eyebrows and clasped my hand over my mouth. Stifling a titter as he frowned and his eyes blazed through me, a wave of chills washed over me only to re-envelope me when he seductively purred, "Or maybe I won't. Maybe right now, I might be in the mood to prefer a badly behaved woman to chastise with a crop or perhaps give a good flogging to!"

Pursing my lips, I spring back from him, raise my palm to him as to halt him from coming near me and muse quietly for a few seconds. "How do you propose to get me so easily controlled?"

He squints, takes a step towards me and coils his fingers around my wrist. "Hand down, Helena."

I flay my arm to my side. Before I can consciously think of another word or action to express how I am feeling, he nudges me hard up against the rail of the bed and as I flop back onto the mattress, within a flash, he has straddled my naked body. "I am going to tame you just like this."

"How are you going to?" I breathe.

"You are going to be pinned beneath me for the duration of our first love-making. You will not change position and when you feel me enter your body you will understand why."

He makes no hesitation in holding back any further and I make no effort to halt him. He begins by cupping my breasts in his hands, and as he sensually circles each pink nipple between his thumbs and forefingers, deftly working me into a place of erotica – *He's weakening me with his touch* – I sink back into the cotton covered mattress and lose myself in his following words:

"You *are* mine, Helena. Always remember that."

I toss my head back, all my defences are down and I'm in serious trouble now. I want him so desperately inside me, yet I still feel that I need to stand my ground with him.

His mouth is now upon my right breast, and his lips are clamped around my tightening bud. While he sucks on my flesh, drawing hard upon it, he releases my other breast from his hold, and settles his warm palm between my legs. Slipping a finger inside me, he probes deep, and on that sensual touch of his, I groan out his name. He pauses, looks up at me, rests his chin upon my chest and flatters, "You like that combo my precious? By the fire in your eyes, I can tell that you are craving so much more of my intimate touches, aren't you?"

I am now aching to the very inner core of my being and whisper a sexy whisper in my voice, I affirm to him that yes, I do indeed want more of his touch. I can't prevent myself from staving him off any further... I truly don't wish to so while I part my legs a little for him, he maintains eye contact with me and slowly inserts his second finger into me. I arch my back and bear down onto him and I wail out a weak no as I feel the aching sensation throbbing within the soft flesh of back wall of my vagina. With a moment, he has done what no other man has ever been able to do to me – he has located my elusive G-spot. Not breaking vision with me, he slowly works me, coaxing the pent up wetness from within me. With my moisture now slicking over his digits, he continues taunting me with a consecutive motion of agonisingly slow rhythmic movements between my legs. With my body writhing, desiring to feel his cock inside me, he halts and with his fingers remaining inside me, he shimmies his body over me and hungrily crushes his alcohol scented lips to mine.

I'm sure within the confines of his deep, lingering kisses, I heard him whisper something about making an honest woman out of me.

Stopping his tease, he withdraws his fingers and places them to my mouth. Lightly pressing them on my lower lip, I double-blink when he softly asks, "Tell me, baby. Tell me why you need to be on birth control."

I am so lost within this moment, that I quietly whisper, "I use it to stop heavy periods."

Everything suddenly goes a hush and he rolls off of me, and reaches out for my hand. I let him take it. He draws me up until I am positioned upright on my knees. Placing my hand to his mouth, he kisses each fingertip in turn and then in a light-hushed tone, he completely melts me when he says,

"No questions now, Helena, for I am taking you to *my* bed."

CHAPTER TWELVE

With me naked and cradled in his arms, Darius raises his right leg and balances on one foot. Not teetering in the slightest, he gently kicks the door to his bedroom. As it falls open, what I see before me completely takes my breath way, for the room is so stark, so pristine it seems to have an almost sterile quality about it. Positioned in the centre of the room is a queen-sized, four poster bed. From each of the corner pelmets drape sumptuous, dark-grey voiles that shimmer in the light. The bed itself is adorned with an array of lavish and opulent pillows. The smaller ones are the purest of virginal white and the larger ones are a contrasting charcoal-grey. There appears to be so many that adorn the pure white cotton sheeting that lies beneath them that I'm sure, one could easily lose themselves within the confines of their lavish abundance. There is a window. Well it's more of a whole glass floor to ceiling wall. It too is elegantly embellished with voiles which complement in colour the ones that are garnishing his bed. Situated on the floor a few feet from the window I note a free standing telescope.

Maybe he's a star-gazer? Maybe he's a lover of all things heavenly bodied?

Stilling, he confidently asks, "Do you like my room, Helena? Tell me what you are thinking."

"I do, Darius. It's erm… erm… I would say very minimalist, but nevertheless it must be an extremely calming place to relax and sleep in."

"It is, indeed both of those," he replies. "And do you want to know something else?"

Now intrigued, I tell him that yes I would.

"Are you sure?"

"Yes."

"No one has ever slept in my bed except me."

"You are serious, Darius? No one at all has ever lain down next to you? You've never had a woman in your bed with you?"

"No… Never." He wistfully breathes.

Amazed at his declaration, I ask, "Can I ask you why?"

"Because…" he momentarily pauses and sighs, "I've never wanted to wake up with a woman by my side until this very moment."

Truly heart warmed at his sentiment, as he settles me down on the bed, he tells me to make myself comfortable, and that because I have aroused him greatly, he is going to need to take a refreshing shower to rebalance his thoughts. While he shimmies out of his sweatpants, he casts them aside, and jaunts off in the direction of what I assume must be his en suite. While I flop back into the cushions, I don't take my vision off those pert, dimpled buttocks of his. He soon disappears out of my view. On hearing water beginning to cascade, my curiosity gets the better of me and I decide to go on a little spying mission. I follow his path. On seeing him standing in what I can only describe as a wet room with his eyes closed, I smile as I watch him all gloriously soapy, his hand circulating the sea-sponge around his torso. Angling his face up to the warm jets of water, while the moisture bounces off his strong jawline, cascades over his broad shoulders, and trails down his back, the muscles that lay beneath his scapula flex and relax. I don't know what came over me, but I stepped into the shower to join him. With no hesitation at all, I wrapped my arms around his midriff and cradled my cheek into his warm back.

"Helena." he groans. "What on earth are you doing?"

Slipping my hand lower with the full intention of touching his cock, he peels my hands from his person and turns around to face me. Snaking his hand around my bare waist, he draws me flush into him. As the warmth of our skin-upon-skin sends shivers cascading down my spine, he gently settles his other hand around the back of my head. As I felt the hairs on the nape of my neck erect, I liquefied even further when he so, so sexily whispered, "Tell me what you are wishing for right now, Helena."

With a certain type of bashful shyness in my voice, and without hesitating, I found myself quietly murmuring to him, "I wish that you would hurry up and kiss me."

He knowingly smiled.

I openly blushed.

Steadying my face in his hands, he leant into me and bestowed one of the most hungering kisses I have ever experienced.

And as he kissed me so deeply, so passionately, and so intensely, I immediately forgot the air that I was breathing. As we let ourselves go and lost ourselves in the sweet tastes of each other's mouths, no words are spoken. There was no need for words.

I am now cajoled up against the shower wall and he is cupping my buttocks in his hands. While he positions me over him, his cock prodding at my centre, I wrap my legs around him. His kisses are deepening and I am left mystified when he hooks one arm under the backs of my knees and scoops me up into his arms. Draping my arms around his neck for support, as he skims his lips along mine, he quietly mumbles, "Not here."

"Then if not here, Darius, where do you propose we should make love?"

As we slowly walk towards the bed, he tickles me when he chuckles, "I've got to move a little slower than usual."

Knowing full well why, I smirk, "Why do you have to move slowly?"

Now chortling away, he answers, "Because you, my little femme fatale have just turned me into a walking tripod!"

"What do you mean a walking tripod?"

"Well it's like this," he laughs, "I have two legs and between them I have an extremely stiff cock that is throbbing away like crazy! Does that answer your question?"

While I fall about into fits of girlish laughter at his description, he settles me down onto the bed. I shuffle up until my shoulders rest upon the cushions. He crawls up the bed and joins me. Aligning his body with mine, he first entwines his fingers with mine. While he pins one arm above my head, he repeats this action with my other. Brushing my lips with his, he divulges to me, "You're changing me, Helena."

"I don't want to transform you, Darius," I honestly say. "I like you just the way you are."

Nuzzling noses, he continues, "Baby, I mean… I… I…"

"Hush," I soothe. "Right now we do not need to speak. All I want to hear is the sound of our bodies moving in unison."

His eyes widen and his irises shimmer with such enticement that I am actually starting to believe that this man who I am beneath might actually be *falling in love with me. – I hope he is.* We are now both kissing each other with such urgency, that we lose ourselves in each other's heartfelt affections. I wrap my legs around him and he responds by slipping his hands underneath my buttocks.

"Condom, Darius?" I murmur.

"No condom," He soothes. "There is no need."

"But the pill is not one hundred per cent reliable."

He stills over me, looks quizzically at me and I hitch a breath when he so softly says,

"I'll take the risk with you, Helena. You are the only woman I would ever take *any* risk for."

Lifting me into him, I let out a breath as the crown of his cock warms against my moist folds. A moan simultaneously escapes from both our lips, and it is consecutively replaced by us both whispering out each other's respective names. With each soft, timely movement of his body inside mine, the passion in his deep-blue eyes coupled with his erotic words cause my soul to liquefy. He's taking me closer to the brink with each slow, rhythmic stroke of his hardness. I nip his upper lip. He responds by releasing an enticing sexy guttural groan. It's the sound that warbles from the back of his throat and my calling his name that sends us both spiralling closer to the edge.

The reason for these cries of ours was because as the tight, pent-up energy we had both held back for the best part of the last few hours had finally reached its channel of release and as he entered my body, I groaned out in a way that I have never done before. The compelling force behind his first thrust, flowed from his lean hips, and he began thrusting into me like a well-oiled piston. Clinging onto his hair for leverage, I whined out his name and as the syllables of his title fell over and over again from my soul, it echoed around this sparsely decorated bedroom of his. He rocked, he gyrated and he ground deeper and deeper into me only momentarily pausing, when his sweat-sheened torso began to show signs of a trembling. Burying his head into the crook of my neck, his damp, silky locks falling against my heated skin, he whispered to me that he knows how close we are both to orgasming, and that he is going to make damn sure that we arrive at that sensuous point together. Stilling, he pushed his palms flush into the pillows that my head was rested upon and beared down upon me.

"I'm so lost inside you, Helena," he soulfully declared and then added. "I'm permanently absorbed within your aura."

Oh my. He's softening?

Close to tears of joy, I gasped a breath and replied, "And I am found when you are inside me."

Whilst he continued devouring my body and claiming my soul with an abundance of passionate, words, with the next upward powerful thrust of his manhood coupled with his finger that was increasing its pressure on my swollen nub, he nipped the sensitive flesh that coats the side of my neck and in between his short, heavy breaths, he lowly purred,

"Do I have you yet, Helena?"

As my body tremored and his did too, as we did indeed share our concurrent releases, I hummed,

"Always, Darius… You will *always* have me."

"Good," he satisfyingly panted and then melted me to the inner core when he affirmed and emphasized the word *always*.

"And you, my precious will *always* belong to me."

A few moments passed by and with his body still covering mine, his voice ragged and raspy, he softly whispered into my ear, "I want to make love with you again, Helena."

On feeling him dragging his warm lips up the soft skin of my neck, he murmured against my damp flesh, "Yet here it is.

It's only been a few moments since we shared our orgasms, and already I'm aching to be moving inside you again."

I gazed up at him with wonderment, and as his eyes misted over, he left me breathless with the following, "when we just made love, it nearly killed me. You've left me craving for so much more of you."

Not breaking eye contact with him, I lightly ran my fingers down his sweat-sheened back, and while his torso shuddered against mine, I quietly whispered, "Why so, Darius?"

"Because," he drew a deep breath, and moved me emotionally when he so soulfully replied, "because I had to battle... I had to try so very hard to fight off my impending climax with every single fibre of my being. How is this possible, baby?" He implored, "please can you tell me."

To which I, without hesitation, pressed my mouth to his and with a braveness in my voice, I honestly answered, "maybe it's because I have become everything to you... maybe we have just become everything to each other."

"Yes, you have. Yes, we have." He sighed, and as he breathed into my mouth. "You are my world." He then began to set a rather slow, timely rhythm between us.

CHAPTER THIRTEEN

Saturday Morning

"And you, my precious will always belong to me."

DARIUS

When we finally release from our first kiss of the day, as the sweet taste of Helena's mouth lingers on my tongue, I am left inebriated from not only the soft touch of her lips but also the warmth of her tongue as it danced around mine. I feel as if I have been sipping on the finest of champagnes and the bubbles have gone straight to my head. I open my eyes and the vision beneath me is a true beauty to wake up to. I gaze down upon her and as she beams me the most beautiful smile a multitude of harmonious new sensations surge through my veins. At an alarming rate they flow freely and as they reach my heart and pierce my soul, without any warning, I find myself free-falling into her encompassing aura. She looks up at me and sweetly asks, "Are you alright, Darius? You seem to be somewhere else."

I roll onto my side, rest on my elbow and cradle my cheek in the palm of my hand "I am, baby. Do you think you find me?"

She creases a little worried frown and tells me that she's confused and she's not sure if she can. I smile at her, give a little chuckle and reassure, "Don't worry, I'll find me."

She manages a half-smile so I slowly start to trace the outline of her heart with my finger. I press lightly into the centre of the invisible template drawn and whisper to her that I am hiding somewhere inside the precious place that is nesting beneath her blood and bones. I am in fact dwelling in her heart and I always will be.

HELENA

On releasing from the first kiss of the day, Darius broke into one of the most enchanting, sleepy smiles I have ever seen emanate from him. Grasping the cotton sheeting tightly in his fist, he drew it over us - completely obscuring us from the stark, morning's sunlight - Next he, in such a secretive tone, whispered, "Did you feel that?"

Gazing lovingly up at him, I questioned, "Feel what?" Spreading my legs with his knee and his cock now nudging at my centre, he amusingly chuckled, "That strangest of sensations that surged through your soul, when we pressed our lips to each other's."

"Oh that." I smiled, "I was wondering as to what it was." Not taking his vision off me, he grinned and slowly entered me. Stilling over me, I wrapped my legs around him, and pleaded with him to make love with me again. The most gentle of looks lit up his face, and he honoured my wish by beginning to set a timely rhythm. In between each one of his to-and-froing strokes, he completely took my breath away when he stared intently at me and smiled, "It was you and I becoming as one."

THE GIFT

Darius takes the breakfast tray from my lap, settles it onto the floor, and then seats himself next to me. Leaning into me, he whispers into my ear that he has a present for me. Asking me to close my eyes, and then cup my hands together, I do one then the other. On feeling something firm settle into my upturned palms, I open my eyelids to see a black box resting in my hands. Looking quizzically at him, smiles and gives me a slow, alluring bat of his long, curly lashes. Now beaming from ear to ear like a Cheshire cat, he gently urges for me to open it.

"What is inside it?"

His smile doesn't alter and he with a hint of amusement in his voice suggests, "Shall we open it together and find out?"

I nod to him that we should, so as I hold the box firm, he wiggles the lid off and tosses it onto the bed. Scrunching back the tissue paper that hides the surprise beneath, he dips his fingers inside and extracts what I can only describe as something velvety and red. Dangling the items up in front of my face, he asks. "Do you know what these are?"

I arch an eyebrow and ask, "Are they by any chance a set of wrist cuffs?"

Leaning into me, he seductively whispers into my ear, "Yes, my precious, they are. And they are going to look absolutely divine wrapped around those petite little wrists of yours."

Shifting back from him, I ask, "You're… you're intending to… to… restrain me?" I stammer.

"As I've mentioned before, Helena, I will never do anything to you that you don't wish for me to do. But if you would like to *play* with me, I'm more than happy to show you the way!"

"What if I say to you that I don't want to be bound?"

He sighs, mumbles to me if that's what you wish and plops the cuffs back into the box. While he fumbles on the bed sheets for the lid, my subconscious blurts out that she thinks she would like to play and therefore could he please hurry up and begin. On hearing my voice, he tickles me to the core, when with such a cheekiness in his voice; asks me if I am ready to embark on said game.

"Mmm," I muse. "And may I ask, sir exactly what type of game did he have in mind?"

He fleetingly raises his eyebrows and answers, "Sir? I like that name very much."

"So?" I jest, "What's the name of the game then, *sir?*"

"It's called," he winks. "I have named it the *triumphant – winner-takes-all*!"

I burst out laughing at his choice of words and before I can blink, he has curled his hands around my ankles and is gripping me firm. I am now being dragged down the bed and with my back flush against the crumpled silk beneath me, as he straddles me, I proclaim, "What on earth are you doing?"

"Well it's like this, Helena. Firstly I am going to secure your arms."

Oh my...

"And secondly if you enjoy this game, afterwards, I'll take you somewhere very, very special."

Where?

Looming over me, he grasps my right wrist in his hand and winds the ties of the cuff around it. On completing the last rotation of the red, velvet ribbon, he pinches the ends between his thumbs and forefingers, deftly fashions it into a knot, yanks it tight and while declaring,

"You are pure perfection, Helena."

I know, Darius.

Securing the ends of said ribbon to the slatted headboard, I lay motionless as he repeats his actions on my other wrist. Resting back on his haunches, he stares intently at me, he flits me a bash lat and then, in such a sexy-honeyed tone, purrs, "Have you ever heard of the Japanese term, 'Kinbaku-bi' Helena?"

Now splayed out on the bed like a virginal offering that is looking up to the heavens for some form of divine direction, I pull against my wrist restraints and as the feeling of a complete lack of power engulfs me, my heart does something mysterious of its own. Drawing in a breath of air, my voice weakens a little and I whimper, "No. I have never heard of that terminology before. What does it mean?"

Trailing his finger along the inside of my thigh, he leans over me, and with his forefinger, he skims along my dampening folds. Now taunting me, teasing me with the lightness of his probing touch, he seductively offers, "It means 'the beauty of tight binding."

"Oh," I exclaim. "So you believe that by binding me tight there is a beauty within this art that you call submission? It arouses you seeing me powerless?"

Shuffling back from me, he dips his head between my legs, holds my thighs firm so I cannot move and blows a light puff of air over my centre. I whimper out his name and he raises his lashes, and whispers, "Yes it does. It really elevates me sexually knowing that you have no influence or control over your body." He then boldly adds, "and if you enjoy this gentlest of teases maybe one day in the future, If you agree to become my submissive, I will show you *exactly* what Kinbaku-bi entails."

With his head now buried between my legs, his hands holding me still, as his tongue bestows upon me a series of erotic slow, delectable licks and flicks, I'm aching to grasp his mop of dark hair and push my lower body into him. He senses this, pauses, looks up at me, shoots me a wink and resumes his sensual onslaught. On bringing me to my climax, I convulse into him, and as wave upon wave of orgasm shatters me to the inner core, I am left with the following thoughts flowing through my mind.

I am now silently admitting to myself that I'm becoming ever closer to deciding whether I want to delve into Darius' world of dominance and submission.

CHAPTER FOURTEEN

Sunday

Five p.m.

As the car halts outside my apartment, Darius switches off the engine and unbuckles my seatbelt. I turn to face him.

"It's going to be a difficult week without you, Helena." he frowns. "This weekend was something I have only ever dreamt about in my wildest dreams. You've really got under my skin and there's not a thing I can do to extract you from my soul."

Stunned at his words, I run my finger along his cheek and while I close my eyes and trace the outline of his jaw, I whisper, "I'm going to miss you too, Darius. I know I will be feeling lost without you in my life."

He settles his hand over mine and I open my eyes. He's now cradling his face in my palm and I almost well up when he so softly says, "I'd much prefer us to be miserable together than miserable apart."

I agree and to ease the uncomfortableness of this separation, I open the car door and step out onto the pavement. Poking my head back into the car, I ask, "Don't get out, Darius. I'll be fine."

"Why, Helena? Why do you want me to stay inside the car? Let me at least show you to your front door. Let me have one more kiss."

"I don't think I could bare it if you touched me again."

"Why?" he looks bemused. "Am I that much of a grotesque of a man?"

"No," I assure. "The reason why I don't wish for you to touch me is that if you did, I would easily fall into your arms and want to stay with you forever."

With relief in his voice, he chirps, "Well that sounds like an excellent plan to me."

I half-smile. "Yes, it does rather, doesn't it?"

He smiles too and I have to reluctantly close the door because the hungering look in his eyes is so magnetically powerful that I have to put a tactile *barrier* between us or I will indeed fling myself at him. Even knowing that we will talk/text during the week, I still feel a strange sense of loss. Because during the past weekend, even though Darius had touched upon the dominance/submissive issue, he never fully thrust the issue upon me. I'm am extremely curious about what D/s entails, so as I climb up the steps to my home, I make a conscious decision that over this forthcoming week, I will do some investigative research upon the latter subject. *Forearmed and forewarned. Best to be prepared*!

Turning, as I see the taillights of his car fading into the distance, I am broken from my thoughts when my cell buzzes. Extracting it from my jacket pocket, as I read the message, my heart takes a multitude of successive flips.

When you step inside your home, the first thing I wish for you to do is to check your mail, Helena.
You should find a large brown envelope that is awaiting your immediate attention.
Missing you already.
Forever yours,
Darius
Xx

That was the first thing I did when I stepped inside my apartment was to check my mail and as Darius had messaged, there was indeed a large brown envelope requiring my attention.

CHAPTER FIFTEEN

MONDAY

Seven-thirty a.m.

Stepping out of the shower, I hear my phone buzz on the vanity unit. Picking it up I see that that Darius has left me a message. This is the conversation that follows:

Helena, after last weekend, I'm finding myself missing you dreadfully. I need to feel your touch upon me once again... I just need all of you.

Me too...

May I ask if you received the envelope and if you have, have you opened it?

Yes I have and yes I did open it.

I hope you're not cross with me for being forthright or with the contents that the dossier contains.

No, not angry at all. I'm just a bit taken aback by both your boldness, and some of the points written among the pages.

May I ask if you have taken the time yet to read the contract?

Yes, I have. I'm a small way in.

And what are your thoughts so far?

I can't text them. They're too sensitive to filter through the airwaves.

That's a shame. I would've loved to have read them but I fully understand how you must be feeling.

Thank you.

On another note, tell me, what are you wearing?

Why do you wish to know?

I'm curious...

Well considering I have just showered and I am thinking about what set of lingerie to wear... nothing.

getting aroused here at the thought of you, damp skin and naked. – show me?

Pardon me?

Text me a photograph of you right this very minute!

Why?

Because I am feeling extremely pervy!

laughing

Not *laughing* – *smirking*

Darius, Can you guess what I'm doing right now?

Lying on your bed with your legs apart while imagining my tongue lapping gently at your naked centre by any chance?

Maybe...

I wish I was doing exactly what I have just suggested.

Darius, are you by any chance seated in your car with your trousers unzipped and your cock in your hand?

That's very forthright, Helena, and I have to say that that is a most erotic suggestion of yours, so give me a moment and I will oblige.

I'm touching myself. My nipples are stiffening at the thought of you stroking your cock!

Damn you, you little tease, Helena. *stiffening eh?* your nipples aren't the only thing that's hardening at this moment for my cock is rock hard and my body's aching for your touch.

Oh...

I really need to release...

Do you?

Oh yes, very much so! So send me a picture of you? I want to climax while ogling your beautiful naked body.

Nope, Mr Pervert. You'll just have to use your vivid imagination!

Do it you little minx because if you don't, when I see you next, I will put you over my knee, pull your panties down and spank your perfectly formed arse until your flesh smarts, and your thighs are quivering for my probing touch.

That sounds like a most excellent idea! I can't wait for that moment!

pitiful voice Talk dirty to me, Helena. I'm fit to burst here!

If I do, what do I get in return?

You will receive the satisfaction that you have made your dominant replete!

Oh... So you really do wish for me to be your submissive?

Yes...

I'll think carefully about it...

Don't take too long perusing over the idea because at present I'm cupping my balls in my hand and stroking my cock with the other. I'm imagining that your mouth is doing some rather delightful things to me....

giggling – *That's very rude, sir...*

not tittering – so... so... close to climaxing – talk erotica to me, baby, please?

Close your eyes and relax back into your seat.

Yes, ma'am!

Ready?

Get on with it Helena!

salutes *Yes... sir!*

You are perfect, baby...

I know.

GO!

Imagine this Darius... I'm sitting right next to you, and as I unbuckle my seatbelt, you hold your cock firm in your hand. I lean over you, dip my head into your lap, and blow a light puff of air over your blood-gorged pole of muscle. You, on feeling my lips fleet along the crown of your throbbing manhood, hiss out my name.

Don't stop for I'm seriously twitching right now!

You are now placing your hand on the back of my head, and gently pushing me down until my lips again sweep across the plump, spongy circumference of your cock. "Suck me, Helena." You breathe through clenched teeth. "I want you to taste me." Is that any good so far, Darius?

*groaning and typing with one very shaky finger while rolling the length of my cock with my free hand! – Do continue...

Slipping my hand into your silk boxers, I start to gently ply your tightening balls, and while I massage them, I curl my fingers around the root of your cock. I am glancing up at you, and as you bear down upon me, by the fiery glaze that's burning in your steely-blue irises, I can tell that you desire for me to take you into my mouth. Your body is now quaking and you are grabbing a fistful of my hair. While you pull it tight, you command me to draw upon you hard, As I do, and I take you as deep as in possibly can, I draw upon your veined muscle, and that is the precise moment when I feel your body start to shudder...

Jeez, baby, my body is racking!

Shhh... Concentrate...

I'm so close...

As your fluid spills into the back of my throat, I hear you growl for me to... to... swallow. I do... A throaty rumble escapes from your lips and I swallow again, just quickly enough before you empty fully. As your body sags, breathing rapid, your grip lessening upon my hair, you coerce me into rising at meeting your mouth. Looking delightfully flushed with tiny beads of moisture glistening above your upper lip, you in-between labouring breaths, sensually ask me to kiss you. I do. It is now that you erotically declare that it will soon be my turn to be pleasured.

One minute later: Darius?

Two minutes later: Darius are you alright?

Four minutes later: Darius have you... you... Erm... hand-fucked yourself almost to death, or are you still alive and breathing?

Eight minutes later: Darius, you're scaring me. Please answer me?

Ten minutes later: I'm here baby.

Why did you take so long to respond?

Well let's just say, by your in depth sexual coaching, I felt extremely drained!

triumphantly giggling here so one could say that you had a rather explosive release?

Indeed I did... So Helena, what are the odds on me sex talking for you?

Would lunch-time today suit you, sir?

You can count on it, and by the way, I still want that photo of you.

One minute later: Helena?

Two minutes later: Helena, talk to me!

Four minutes later: Helena, you're making me anxious. Where are you?

Eight minutes later: Helena, answer me or I'll come over and spank you!

Ten minutes later.

Pressing send...

Nice photo!

Good... hopefully it will keep you satisfied until our next chat!

You're making my cock twitch again... Damn you, woman... I just want to be inside you...

I wish you were here...

Be careful what you desire for, Helena.

Why?

Just because...

I have to go now... Get ready for work... Or I'll be dreadfully late.

Ditto... sadly... Until lunchtime my little femme fatale...

Until lunchtime, Mr Carter!

CHAPTER SIXTEEN

Monday

The Florists

Picking up my phone, I see that I have one new message. The sender is Darius, and this is the conversation that followed.

"Turn around, Helena."

"Excuse me?"

"I said, turn around!"

"Why?"

"Because I want you to."

"That's a ridiculous answer."

"If you turn around, you will see that it's not such a daft request after all."

sighing "All right, I'm turning."

"Good..."

On hearing the lock click on the door to the shop, I spin around to see Darius standing in the doorway. Dropping the bouquet of peonies and lilies to the floor, now rooted to the spot, I stammer, "Darius. What... what on earth are you doing here?"

Beaming me an alluring smile, one that he knows will captivate my attention, he shrugs out of his grey suit jacket, tosses it onto the countertop, and boldly strides towards me. On reaching me, I shudder as he makes no hesitation in snaking his hand around the back of my neck. Drawing me into him while the scent of his manliness invades and infuses my sense, I liquefy inside as he so lowly whispers, "Well after this morning's texting shenanigans, I thought I it would only be polite if I came over to see you and reward you for your kind assistance in making me temporarily replete."

Now lightly nibbling my ear lobe as he murmurs what he would like to do to me in the back room before the lunch hour is over, I feel my head beginning to spin followed by knees weakening.

"Darius, please stop," I pine. "We're in my place of work and Angelica will be back any moment."

Now running his tongue along the side of my neck, while I falter further, he asks, "Really… What makes you think she'll be back shortly?"

Now faltering under his touch, I moan, "I just… just know she will."

Pushing his torso into me, while I feel his cock, stiff and rigid prodding against my belly, I drape my arms around his neck. Holding onto him for support, I rise onto my tippy-toes, and seek out his mouth. As his lips meet mine, he brushing his lips along mine and sensually murmurs, "I think you may be wrong about that, Helena," he grumbles.

"Why?" I mewl in response.

"Because," he pauses, and then melts me even further by dipping his tongue into my mouth, sliding his hands down my back until they settle on my buttocks and giving me a hard slap.

Jolting into him, I beg, "Darius, please stop… This is far too risky."

Cupping my arse in his hands, he gives it a soothing stroke and growls, "I won't stop. I love taking risks especially with you and as I'm going to have you within the next few moments, I suggest you relax and let me have what I want."

He slaps me again and as the stinging sensation radiates through my skirt and my panties dampen, I whisper, "What, what about Angelica… she… she… "

Lifting me up, I instinctively clasp my legs around him and with me clamped around his midriff, he begins to walk toward the back room. As we enter, he begins ferociously kissing me with such urgency that I am fast becoming breathless. In between his breaths he tells me to stop worrying about Angelica because he texted her this morning and suggested if she'd like to have lunch with his brother.

Did I hear him right? He has a brother?

"You have a brother?"

"Yes, I do," he sighs, "but now we don't need to talk anymore because *I am* now going to pleasure us both."

With my back now up against the wall, if I wanted to speak I couldn't for he is crushing his lips on mine while rashly unzipping his trousers. Within a flash, he has roughly pushed up my skirt and yanked my very *safe* Marks and Spencer's white cotton panties to one side. Probing me with his finger, he drawls into my ear, "Although I love the fact you're already wet for me, I have to tell you that I am not quite so exuberant about your choice of underwear."

"Sorry," I squeak.

He breathes a low throaty-rumble into my mouth and while he chants my name over and over, I cry out for him. He glares hard at me, slides two fingers between my folds and presses down on the back wall of my aching core. Within an instance he has deftly located my sensitive spot and I am clasping him tight. While I plead with him to be quick, he deviously chuckles and stuns me by asking, "Considering you are so beautifully moist for me, I'm guessing that your panties have been equally damp after our sex texts this morning?"

I dig my nails down into his shoulders, whimper out a *probably*. He arouses me even further when he grabs the side of my underwear in his fist and blurts,

"I detest these fucking sensible panties of yours. You shouldn't wear such unflattering underwear."

Biting the corner of my lower lip, I in the tiniest of voices say, "They're practical."

"Practical or not," he hisses, "I should rip them off you."

We're now at stalemate and I probe, "You wouldn't dare do such a thing, would you?"

Cocking an eyebrow at me, he frowns, and the dark, smouldering glint in his irises causes me to shiver. Tightening his grip on said panties, he leers in a little closer, if it was at all possible and rasps, "Oh wouldn't I?"

"No, you wouldn't." I jest and then simper, "Would you?"

He just did!

Ow!

Pressing his lips to mine, he speaks, "Shhh, precious, you know you should never challenge your master when he is in his alpha mode, don't you?"

Digging my nails deeper into the roundness of his shoulders, I murmur out an *Mmm.* Yes, sir. He then smirks and asks, "That wasn't uncomfortable really, was it?"

"Yes, it was a tiny bit."

Not questioning me any further, he slips his hand underneath my arse, lifts me down onto him and as he inches his cock into me, my back thumps against the cold, stone wall.

"Tell me, Helena," he breathes, "promise me that you will always be mine."

With him now setting a slow and timely rhythm, his cock filling me inch by inch, and stretching me, it takes no time for our bodies to rack over each other's and as my pent up cum slicks over his cock and one of the most powerful climaxes I have ever encountered spears through my centre, it quivers me to the very core. As his body does too, I without shame, wail extremely loudly, that I will always be his. He grumbles a *good.* My body responds by going limp and I collapse into his heaving chest. Still entwined, we slump to the floor, and he cradles me in his arms. Stroking my hair, while our breathings begin to labour I am left agog when he slides out of me, rests up on his haunches and holds up my shredded *not-so-sensible panties-anymore* up in front of my face. Placing them to his nose, he deeply inhales and without a hint of embarrassment in his voice, he says, "The musky scent of you is so damn alluring, so sexy. I could easily go again!"

Now both amazed and amused at his *après-wall-bang humour*, I playfully swat him and tell him that he is most definitely a grade one pervert. Grasping his now softening cock, he gives it a hard squeeze, laughs and then muses, "Maybe I am or maybe my cock has a mind all of its very own!"

"Pray a heaven that is doesn't. I don't think that I could keep up with you if it did!"

Tucking himself away, he zips up his trousers and rises to his feet. Offering me his hand, I take it and say,

"I need to go to the bathroom. I desperately need to pee."

"Can I come too?" he wickedly suggests.

"No way can you, Mr Carter," I giggle. "Ladies first, so you can go after me."

Tipping his finger under my chin, he tilts my face upwards, skims his lips along mine and murmurs,

"That's a crying shame for I would've loved to watch you…"

I press my lips to his and silence him with a kiss for, right now, at this particular moment in time; I didn't want nor need to hear the end of his sentence.

CHAPTER SEVENTEEN

TUESDAY

As my phone alerts me that I have one new message, I settle my tea cup back onto its saucer, and pick up my cell from the countertop. The sender again is Darius and this is how the conversation unfolded.

"Thank you for yesterday, Helena."

I reply, "My pleasure, Mr Carter."

"No thank you, Helena and I can assure you that the pleasure was all mine."

"If you say so..."

"I do and I am missing you dreadfully. I dreamed of you last night, and this morning too. I have to say; at least your panties kept me company while I was all alone!"

Without hesitation I quickly text back, "Pervert!"

"Always! ... Have you read anymore of the contract?"

"Yes."

"And?"

"My thoughts are still too delicate to text."

"Shame for I would've loved to have read them. They would've kept me going until Friday arrived."

"Sorry, still no can do."

"There's no need for sorry. Can I see you today?"

"No."

"What! Why?"

"I need to digest, assess what is happening to me... to us."

"Are you fobbing me off? Am I not good enough for you? Do you wish you we dating someone else?"

"None of the above... I just need a little breather."

"Why?"

"Because everything's been happening so very fast."

Reluctantly texting "I think I understand what you are trying to say."

"I really have to go, Darius. My work calls. Speak tomorrow?

"Yes, we will."

"Goodbye for now."

"Sadly... goodbye for now, Helena."

WEDNESDAY

Lying on my bed with the contract splayed out in front of me, as I turn the fourth to last page, my phone alerts me that I have one new message. – Darius. This again is how the conversation unravelled.

"I really need/want to see you, Helena. I'm aching to the inner core for your touch."

"Me too, Darius..."

"Have you by any chance reached the end of the read yet?"

"No, not quite..."

"And?"

"I'm pondering."

"Care to elaborate?"

"I will when we meet again on Friday evening.

I wish it was Friday evening now."

"Me too..."

Come over?"

"No can do."

"Why?"

"I'm still assessing you, me... us."

"You're not planning to leave me are you?"

sighing "No, Darius, I'm not working out whether to leave you or..."

"Or what? Finish you statement, Helena! Please don't leave me hanging... that's far too cruel."

"Or stay with you."

"Stay? Forever with me?"

"I'll think about it. I have to go."

"Me too..."

THURSDAY

Ruffling my damp hair with a towel, I stare into the mirror ahead. As thoughts of Darius flood my mind, (I'm constantly thinking of him) the sound of my phone alerting me to a new message breaks my dreamy thoughts of him. On seeing that I have one new message, and the sender is Darius, I smile warmly to myself and take a breath. This is how the conversation unfolded.

"I can't wait to see you tomorrow, precious."

"Me too, Darius. I'm counting down the seconds, minutes and hours."

"Ditto. Have you turned the last page yet?"

"Yes."

"And?"

"I have numerous questions to ask you."

"Good. I would've been disappointed if you didn't have any."

"Darius?"

"Yes, Helena."

"You would never mentally or physically hurt me, would you?"

aghast here! "Absolutely not... Never! Why do you feel the need to ask me this?"

"It... It doesn't matter. Forget it. I'll see you tomorrow."

"It does matter. Everything you do, say and feel matters extremely deeply to me."

"Really?" It does?"

"Truthfully it does."

"I have to go now."

"I wish you didn't. I could talk with you for hours."

"Me too..."

"Until tomorrow then, my Helena."

"Bye, Darius.

"Goodbye, Helena."

CHAPTER EIGHTEEN

Friday Night

While the elevator jerks to a halt, I take a deep breath and stare directly ahead. As the door slides open and Darius comes into my view, my grip tightens on the handles of my holdall that contains my weekend capsule wardrobe. I step out into the private foyer. Stilling, I survey him. I must say, he looks absolutely heavenly dressed in a white crisp shirt that is four buttons open. Seeing a patch of dark, chest hair peeking at me, I tremble inside. Travelling my vision lower, I pass his midriff and the faded ripped jeans that are clinging to his muscular thighs, and halt when I reach his bare feet. As I firmly transfix my vision upon his toes, I hear him ask me to look up at him. I do exactly that. He's now padding towards me and I am firmly rooted to the spot.

On reaching me, he places his hand over mine and I release the hold on my bag. He takes it from me while amusing, "What on earth have you got in here, Helena? By the weight of it, anyone would think that you have come to stay for the duration of your days and not for a lone weekend!"

"Maybe I have come to stay forever with you,"

Dropping said holdall to the floor, he snakes one hand around the back of my neck, and the other hand around my waist. Skimming his lips lightly along mine, he dreamily murmurs, "Imagine that... You, here with me forever, and ever."

Just the mere thought of never having to leave him fills me with a mixture of excitement and hope and I say, "Wouldn't that just be perfect, Darius? Me. Here with you, for eternity?"

He doesn't reply. He just presses his lips lightly to mine, passes the briefest but delicately empowering of kisses upon me. Next, he reaches down and picks up my bag. Offering me his free hand, I accept and without another word spoken, we walk in the direction of his apartment. On stepping inside, my holdall is placed upon the floor and I am led through the lounge and down a spiral staircase that I never noticed on my previous visit.

"Where are we going?"

"We are going somewhere very, very special, Helena. A place that I hope over time you will come to see as *ours*."

Reaching the bottom of said staircase, he turns to face me. Staring intently at me, my eyes widen when he fumbles abound in his jean pocket, locates what he is searching for and dangles the item in front of my face.

"Turn around." He orders. "I am going to blindfold you."

I do. He does.

After my vision has been obscured, he again takes my hand and we walk slowly.

"Where are we going?" I repeat.

He doesn't offer a destination; he just answers me next when I assume that we have arrived at *our* place.

Sliding the velvet blindfold from around my head, he asks me to keep my eyelids closed for just a bit little longer. I oblige. Next, as I feel him settle his palm upon the curve of my lower back, I quiver at the delicacy of his touch.

He then, with a hint of naughtiness within his voice, calmly suggests, "You may open your pretty little eyes now."

As I flick my lashes open, he is already bestowing the lightest of shoves upon my person.

"After you, Helena," he breathes.

His voice appears to be becoming softer than of usual. I wonder as to why.

Taking a small step forth, when I see the room lain out before me, I still, for not only is it the alluring fragrance which I have yet to pin point, infused within the air that is enticing me in, it's also the abundance of candlelight shadows that are causing me to draw in a gasp of a breath. While I stand stiff, I amaze at the flickering silhouettes to and froing upon the bare walls, and something makes me want to look upwards towards the ceiling. *Oh my, oh my what on earth are those objects suspended from the intricate weave of the upper inside surface of this room? Are they collections of objet d'art?* Feeling a little unnerved, and a little embarrassed at not knowing what they might be, I quickly avert my gaze to the floor beneath my feet. It is so highly polished, too shined I think. As I see my shocked reflection mirrored back at me, I am broken from my confusion when I am alerted by his voice rolling through what I have now deciphered to be the scent of ylang-ylang.

"Helena," he without prompt then adds, "One of the acts that a dominant should never perform on his submissive is to suspend her from the ceiling by her wrists alone. The reason being it is impossible to do such an act to a person without causing strain, pain or injury to the submissive in play. D/s is not, and I emphasize not about causing excessive hurt to the one you honour and cherish. There is so much more to D/s that meets the uneducated eye. Do you understand what I am informing you of?"

I just nod as to signal 'yes', for there is not a single word I can find to express how I am feeling at this particular moment in time. Suddenly, I am whirled around and he is tipping his finger under my chin. While I gaze into his eyes, he focuses intently upon me and as I hear him say, "If I was so lucky to have you bound this way," he simpers, "your body would be supported beneath you either by a cushioned footstool or if not that, then I will most definitely be cradling you within my arms."

On hearing his words, something peculiar washes over me and I reply, "If... If...I agree to... to…" I stutter, "To... to…"

"To what?" he gently coaxes.

"To, sign your contract, to be the submissive you appear to be craving for…"

"Yes?"

"Will you keep me safe?"

"Always… I promise."

I can't believe that I am now seriously considering entering his world and as I go to respond, he weakens me further by brushing his lips along mine. Pressing his body into mine, he prises my lips apart with his tongue, and I am lost within the depth of his kisses. When finally he lets me come up for air, he breaks into what I can only describe as a triumphant, knowing smile and then completely stuns me when he tells me that through that kiss, he's sure he heard me verbally agree to become his submissive and that before we may act upon it, there is a small matter of housekeeping that we both must to attend to.

"Housekeeping?" I amaze. "What on earth do you mean? You want me to wash the dishes, make the bed and put the trash out? Those type of duties?"

On hearing my words, he falls about into melodious laughter and softly answers that no, it is not domestic duties that he wishes us to attend to; it is in fact the paperwork that will involve clear, concise reading before finally signing upon.

Oh – Yes – How silly of me not to understand! I almost forgot – The blessed contract!

With the all-important dossier now in front of him, without taking his vision off me, Darius rolls back his cuffs, pushes them up his arms so they squash up just above the elbows, leans forward and rests upon the table. Entwining his fingers, he continues staring intently at me, and then without a single flinch, he launches into one of the most mind-boggling speeches I have heard to date.

"Helena, if you agree to become my submissive, I will show you that there is and always will be room for delicacy within dominance. Believe me when I say that it's not all about hard hands impacting on soft skin or neither is it about firm bindings and intensive restraints that leave their impressions upon ones flesh. For me," he pauses and then continues, "it is about trust and loyalty between two people."

I gasp out at his words. In response to my sound, he frowns and unknots his hands. Tapping a finger on the file, he slides said dossier over to me. As it timely halts in front of me, he completely takes my breath away when he, in a clear and concise tone declares, "I promise you, as your dominant, when you become *my submissive,* when I touch you for the very first time, and my hand slides between your trembling thighs – *They're already quivering, Darius* – I will assert myself tenderly upon your person. As you feel my fingers brushing against your naked centre, I will slowly arouse you in a way like you have never felt before. You will find yourself soon aching to taste the sweetness that I have just extracted from you. When you ask for this, I will honour you by cradling you in my arms and sliding a finger in your mouth. – *Oh good grief!* – And then I will take extreme pleasure from watching your eyes alight as you relish in the heavenly taste of yourself."

As my jaw gapes, he narrows his gaze, slowly bats his long dark lashes at me, and softly whispers, "You see, my precious, it's all about knowing when to build up to a crescendo. Our sexual orchestra will always require punctuating but an exclamation mark, must always be used sparingly."

Unsure of what he means by the latter, I decide that I will add it to my list of questions about the contract and save that ask for later.

"Well, when do we begin to make sweet music?" I jest.

His facial expression doesn't alter; it remains stern, professional and rather business like. I begin to feel a little foolish for making light of his declaration. Pushing back his chair, he languishes back into the leather seating and rests his arms upon his chest. Rocking back and forth, he rolls his eyes to the heavens and speaks to the ceiling, and I am informed that us/the contract is not merely a game. There are no winners and no losers – only players. Next, he looks in my direction, places his hands upon the edge of the table, and draws his chair forward. Glaring hard at me, he states,

"Helena, what I am proposing for us is much more than just a passing amusement, a perverse frolic or a challenge of the sexes. It is and will be a love-affair of our minds, the bodies and ultimately our souls."

"I'm sorry, Darius," I say. "I promise that I will be business-like for the rest of the *reading.*"

He nods as to accept my apology and asks me to open the dossier. I do. "So you told me you have questions, Helena." he proceeds. "I am ready to hear every single one of them. Please begin."

On seeing the black words on the white page, all of a sudden they converge into something unreadable and I quickly snap the dossier shut. Placing my head in my hands, I stare down at the file beneath me and mutter, *I can't do this.*

Moments pass by and as I feel my ponytail being swept to one side and the warmth of his lips brushing against the nape of my neck, his words of encouragement whisper, "You can do this, Helena, otherwise why would you be here?"

I want to tell him that the reason I am here because I am in love with him but now would not be the right time to divulge such an important emotion, so I regained my composure and decided that it was now or never – *now won.* Picking up the Mont Blanc pen, I opened the dossier, turned to the last page and without hesitation, I inked my signature onto the dotted line where indicated. This moment became even more surreal when Darius stopped planting a series of peppery kisses upon my person, leant over me and extracted the pen from between my trembling fingers. Now scribing his signature just below mine, I sagged back into my chair and wondered what on earth I had just done. The dossier was then closed and the pen settled upon the cover. My chair was spun around and I was offered his hand. Accepting it, I rose to my feet. What happened next not only completely caught me off guard but surprised me beyond belief. I was canoodled within his embrace and as he held me there he kept telling me over and over how grateful he was that I had finally become his and that he would do everything within his power to make me the happiest woman on the planet. Drawing back from me, he then asked me to pass him the contract. I gingerly picked it up from the table and passed it over to him. To my utter amazement I watched, my eyes agog like a rabbit that was caught in the headlights of an oncoming car, him, hold the contract up high and swiftly tear it in half and in half again.

My mind now in a whirlwind of emotions, I exclaimed, "Why… Why on earth did you just do that? It took a hell of a lot of courage for me to read it let alone sign it."

Letting the ripped pages float to the floor, he then looked at me, half smiled and told me that said contract was in fact a test. An evaluation of how much I was willing to put my own trust in him and since I have done, he no longer feels it is either worthy or necessary to have such a binding oath between us. I'm more than stunned, when he adds, that the only written oath between a man and woman should be one made within the confines of a church. I am now positively filled with a barrage of unanswered questions and as my tears break forth and begin to rain down my cheeks, he steps in towards me, pulls me into his chest and informs me that he is not going to introduce me to my first lesson in the art of submission at present, he in fact is now going to take me to *our* bed and show me just how much he adores and worships me.

I am now left completely breathless and wanting.

CHAPTER NINETEEN

Saturday Morning

Darius spoons into me, curls his arms around me and I let out a sleepy yawn.

"Good morning, precious," he murmurs. "I trust you slept well."

I press my body into his and reply, "Mmm, I did. I slept very well indeed. And you?"

Nibbling my earlobe, he murmurs, "Same because all that sexual activity left me rather drowsy but now I am awake and so is my cock, I'm waking up nicely."

I force my eyelids open and shuffle around to meet him. He breaks into a broad smile, gently grasps my hand and settles it between his thighs.

"See," he laughs. "I'm awake!"

While I give his semi-erection a light squeeze, he groans at my touch and amuses me when he suggests, "My cock and I think you should hop on top of me and give your master his morning pleasure!"

Giggling at the thought of *hopping on* him, I ask, "If I do perform such an act on you, my *master*, what do I get in return? And don't say me, that *has* become so cliché of late!"

He frowns, muses a little too long for my liking and then captivates my attention when he tells me that my reward will be bestowed upon me tonight. While I coax his manhood into a rigid hardness, I kiss him on the tip of his nose and ask, "Oh and why tonight?"

He strokes the side of my cheek with his finger, and flummoxes me with the following reply. "Because with night comes dark and within the darkness we need a certain type of light to guide us."

With his cock now pulsating away in my hand, I trail my finger along the prominent vein that is now bulging. He closes his eyes, groans out for me to touch him again in that manner and as I do, in in a sweet, sorrowful voice, I ask, "I don't understand, Darius. Could you enlighten me further?"

"Hurry up and straddle me and then I'll explain."

"You promise, master?" I jest. "You promise to me that you will explain?"

With urgency in his voice he answers, "Yes!!" and then hisses, "For pity's sake, Helena, in case you haven't noticed, I'm about fit to burst here."

"Really, you're going to erupt in my hand?"

"By the sensuous way you're stroking my dick like it's some kind of well-earned prize, I swear to you I *am* going to release hard and fast in your hand in a matter of moments!"

Now milking him hard but slow, I tease. "Oh well, we wouldn't want that would we? I mean, me not feeling your morning's hot-pent up offering inside me!"

"Helena!" he rasps. "Stop taunting me... I'm so very close!"

I quickly align my body with his, and as he grasps my hips, he sinks me down onto his cock. With one rotation of his hips, he grinds forcefully into me and I fall forward, flopping against his chest. With my palms now flush to the pillow and my mouth crushing to his, he deftly flips me over, locks me rigid with his body weight and powers into me at an alarming rate. With his torso now trembling over mine, and his warm fluid saturating me, I breathe into his damp neck, "Wow, baby, that was extremely quick."

"Sorry." He sheepishly mumbles into the pillow beneath me. "I couldn't help myself."

"It's all right." I smile.

"Sure?"

"Sure."

Rolling off me he flops onto his back and places his hands behind the back of his head. With his cock still gaily twitching away, in between his labouring breaths, he speaks, "So as I said previously, because with night comes dark and within the darkness we need light, we therefore will need candlelight."

Rolling to face him, I trail my finger down the centre of his heaving chest. "Come on, Mr Riddle, and explain."

"This evening, I would like to *meet* you in my personal room of pleasure. There are three things I wish you to do while you are in there. One: light every single candle that you see. Two: Choose from my vast collection of *toys,* an implement that intrigues you – crop, *flogger,* paddle, whichever is no matter to me – I adore all of them. The decision is yours. And three, when you have done these two tasks, I want you to go back upstairs, shower and return to the room wearing only a pair of heels that I will leave out for you. When you re-enter the room, I expect to see you naked, kneeling and with said implement resting in the palms of your outstretched hands. Do you understand me, Helena?"

"Yes, Mr Carter." I laugh. "I fully understand."

A wry smile broadens across his face and he amazes me when he declares, "Helena, I am going to train you to become the most perfect submissive, I have ever *had.* And ever will have. You will be the ultimate challenge for me. There will never be another woman for me. The only woman for me is you."

He's had a line of submissives before me? Where am I in that line, second, third, tenth, eleventh, nineteenth, twentieth?

CHAPTER TWENTY

Saturday Evening

I wish to saturate my one and only submissive in words of poetic rapture. She's so precious. My loins are aching for the moment when she will allow our bodies to move in unison. I want to imprint love notes on her delicate skin with each timely nip of my teeth and I'm craving to write with my tongue upon her trembling flesh. I desire to be allowed to let my soul flow freely from my mind. While my darkest, innermost thoughts seep through my veins, it will trail unbroken messages of passion behind it... Each heartfelt letter will infuse through my wrists and they will collate between my thumb and forefinger. I desire to trace the curve of her spine with my invisible inscriptions and I wish to leave pearlesque trails of my warm fluid upon her sweat-soaked skin. They will forever be indelible secrets that I have never shared with another. I will leave cryptic messages behind... Little bruises of memos that can never be erased, and when I taste her for the first time it will be like reading an unbroken script. While I am lost in sweet infusions of her mouth, the lines merge until all twenty-six letters converge into one and spell out her name...

...Helena.

THE PADDLE

As Instructed earlier, I did the three things that Darius had requested and now this is what followed.

With my front now flush on something that I can only describe as a bespoke chaise lounge which has been specifically designed/moulded for sexual activities, Darius suggested that I should lay on my front, rest my head upon the pillow at the top end, and raise my buttocks in the air. I did as he expressed and as the coolness of the maroon coloured leather beneath me chilled my body, I felt something soft being wound around my left ankle, and then in turn my right. As the *bind* was yanked tight, I turned my head and I had to catch my breath when I saw Darius and my erotic reflection for the first time in the mirrored wall.

She most definitely wasn't reminiscent of me at all, and may I add, neither was he.

He didn't appear to resemble himself either for even in the soft flickering light of the candles, his face appeared to me to be etched with a severe hardness. I noticed as he clenched his teeth, a prominent muscle on his left jawline spasmed intermittently – *I can only assume that the reason for this facial tick is that he must be deep in some form of hypnotic concentration.* His chest was bare and the only item of clothing he was wearing was a pair of soft, ripped denim jeans that I must admit, over time I become rather fond of witnessing him in. On this occasion, I noticed that there were four buttons open which enabled said jeans to easily drape off his lean hips in such a manner that one could be forgiven for wanting to forget my first lesson in the art of submission and instead turn around, lunge out at him and disrobe him.

Leaning over me, he swept my ponytail to one side and quietly breathed into my ear, "You look so alluring. You are a picture of pure perfection with your ankles bound and your feet graced with my choice of footwear."

He then began caressing my calves, which was the point when his sexual teasing of an onslaught began and I without realising evolved into *his* submissive.

His scented, oiled hands began travelling at an incredible speed over my body and he teased me in a vast array of sexual ways. For the two hours that followed, he had me earnestly pleading with him to penetrate my body. His fingers were probing me, searching me and stretching me in a multitude of undiscovered and unchartered places. Each one opened like a flower in its first innocent blossom and they welcomed his fervent, frantic intrusions with their fragrant but silent aroma. I was so lost within those intense moments of soft erotica that when he whispered to me over and over that I must tell him that I will never leave him; I let my soul run free and told him something that caused him to release his hands from me. His reaction was as if he had just been stung by a swarm of angry bees. He firmly ordered me to bury my head in the pillow, so I did. Moments passed me by and I heard the opening of a drawer. Not daring to turn and see what he was doing, I quivered as his hands suddenly touched the back of my head. The world went dark and the hairs on my skin erected as the soft velvet went to work and obscured the light that surrounded me.

Leaning over me, the heat of his bare chest warming my naked skin, he seductively whispered into my ear, "How do you feel without your vision, Helena? You may speak."

I told him that I felt a little uneasy but also at the same time I was finding myself somewhat intrigued at having to rely on my other four senses. That was the moment when his warmth left my body and I heard the padding of bare feet fading into the distance, followed by the closing of a door. I found myself left bathed in the eeriest of silences. He didn't return for quite a while and I knew that if I moved, he would instantly know. 'How?' you ask? Well, when I first entered this room, I scrutinised it so carefully, and for the briefest of seconds my vision fell upon a video camera suspended in the left corner of the mirrored ceiling. *Kinky devil, Darius!*

On returning, I heard his voice from a distance. "What's your opinion on being filmed, Helena?"

With the lower part of my spine now aching, I wanted to ask if I could change position but knowing that wouldn't do, to ask, I answered, "It excites me, Mr Carter."

A satisfactory noise fell from the back of his throat and I heard him walking towards me. Within seconds his breath was now so close to the side of my neck that as his freshly bathed scent infused my senses, he aroused me even further by asking, "Do you like breathing in the fragrance of your own sex, Helena? Do you like the fact that it has been an hour since I last touched you and your exotic flavour is still lingering upon my tongue? You may answer me."

"Yes, I do… it does something to me…"

His voice firm, he slapped me hard on the arse and growled, "Does something to me, Helena? I think you may have forgotten to finish your sentence."

"It does something to me, *Mr Carter*." I add.

Another sharp slap follows and as he informs me that if I forget my manners again, this lesson will be null and void. I quickly reply *I understand, Mr Carter* and the lesson resumes.

He's now firmly ordering me to place my hands behind my back and he's placing one upturned hand in the other and that is the moment when I hear him murmur, "You are going enjoy this part of the lesson, my precious."

I became so heightened by the thought of us being filmed that I didn't realise my wrists were being cuffed until I heard the sound of the click of a lock. I felt a tugging at my hair and I assumed that he must be winding my tresses around his hand.

Kissing me lightly on the back of my neck, I shivered. The kiss was followed by another sharp sting that radiated across my buttocks. At the intensity of it, I jolted forward, and he started rubbing my now warming cheek, but this time, I didn't feel the comfort of his warm skin upon mine; instead I felt something like soft, leather begin to slip and caress me between my thighs.

"We need a safe word for this part of our game. I think in light of our recent chess game, we should use… checkmate. Nod if you agree."

I nodded.

"You like that, don't you, my angel?" he murmured, "me rubbing you between your quivering thighs? You may answer me."

"Mmm, I do."

"Good… Now you may now count out loud after each impact of your chosen implement."

One… Two…Three… Smack!

His voice rising, he demanded, "Say it, Helena! Say *one*, and after you have, I want you to ask me to continue."

"One – please smack me again, Mr Carter."

"Well done. I am very pleased you called me Mr Carter," he softly praises, "now let's see if we can make it all the way to the glorious number ten."

"Two" – oh my! That feels so good and I have an overwhelming desire to scream for him to quickly do it again,

"Three" – the heat was bearable and pleasurable at the same time.

"Four" – the adrenaline was seeping into my venous system at an alarming rate and I was feeling so turned on.

"Five" – his breathing was deepening and he was making a carnal sound. It's a grunt that I've never heard expressed from a man before.

"Six" – he's nipped me on my shoulder while praising me for making it over halfway.

"Seven" – Ow! That was *really* hard… almost too hard.

"Eight" – I didn't think I could take much more and – *Checkmate* fleeted through my mind and almost rolled off my moisture starved lips.

"Nine. Please… please stop."

"Safe word, Helena," he demanded. "Say it and I promise you I will stop!"

I held back my word of safety and he asked, "No? Then I shall continue… just one more strike and then we have baseline of ten to improve on in the future."

"Ten" – my thighs were aching and every nerve ending that I possessed was positively burning, screaming out for him to probe me with his fingers and to let me climax. On the tenth contact of the paddle, as the red-hot pain seared through my stinging, dry skin, I tried so hard to stop myself from showing him that I couldn't take any more and as the wetness that was pooling between my thighs threatened to release of its own accord, I managed a whimper of desperate plea for him to please let me release. He didn't chastise me for asking. That really did surprise me. On hearing him drop the paddle to the marbled floor and a sense of relief filled me. Next, I heard the unzipping of his jeans and I shifted slightly as he leant over me and whispered that because I had been such a patient and quick learner it was now time for my reward. He informed that I must not climax until he has. The next sounds I heard were the groans and grunt of a man in the rapid throes of what I can only describe as self-pleasuring, and the next sensation I felt upon my body completely took my breath away. A warm fluid splattered onto my buttocks and the primeval, carnal moan that escaped from deep within his throat was positively enthralling to say the least. I cried out for him and as a few drops of my own warm, pent-up moisture started to escape and drip down my inner thighs, he roughly parted my legs and gave what I can only describe as an unsatisfactory low inarticulate sound. He then informed that I still have a lot of patience to learn to control but considering that this was my first lesson, he will choose to ignore my *disobedience.*

How generous of him!

Removing my blindfold, he gently toyed with my pony-tail and asked me to turn and look at him. I did. The quizzical look upon his face excited me even further and when he cupped my centre in his palm, briefly massaging my swollen nub, I mewled as he slowly slipped two fingers into me. As they pressed upon my now expanding bladder, I couldn't hold back any longer and as sweet release drained from my aching body, he sucked hard upon the flesh of my neck, informing me that he was actually leaving secret love notes buried within the deepest layers of my skin. His words not only propelled me into one of the most earth-shattering orgasms I had ever experienced with him, but they also left me intrigued as to who this darker side of him may truly be.

"You are perfect, sweetheart," he soothes. "You are just pure, innocent perfection and you are mine."

While I lay panting, and expressing that I really did need to pee, he quickly released me from my restraints, and lifted me into his arms. Whilst carrying me out of the room, he then informed me that after I had relieved myself we were going to bathe together.

As Darius lowers me into the warm scented water, the first slight of the liquid against my buttocks causes me to let out a little yelp. Lifting me up, he hovers me over the bath, and in a concerned tone asks, "Is that too hot for you, Helena?"

"No, it's fine," I reply. "It's just stinging a little on my bottom."

"I'm sorry it smarts," he sheepishly replies. "I'll soothe it for you later with some of my 'magic' body crème."

I'm puzzled at what he means, but nevertheless I manage to show to that I am amused. Fully immersing my body into the tub, and as I become accommodated with the tingles of light pain that are radiating across my cheeks, he tells me that next time he spanks me, he'll go a little easier on me. While the light scented water swathes my aching body, he says, "Stay with me, Helena. I have so much more to teach you and surely you can see how compatible we are becoming."

He begins to massage my shoulders, and even though the water is warm, I shiver beneath the jasmine scented bubbles.

"Will you stay with me?" he asks again and then adds, "forever."

I tilt my head backwards and close my eyes, digesting that he asked forever.

Stepping into the bath, he aligns his body with mine. With the full weight of his body, he's pinning me down to the tub and the way he's started teasing me, taunting me with his hardness is driving me to point of a wild, crazed insanity.

"Will you stay?"

"I… I… I'm not sure."

"Stay and I'll stop teasing you."

"Maybe I don't want you to stop teasing me."

"You're impossible," he grumbles. "I am going to have to work extremely hard in trying to tame you!"

I laugh but he doesn't join in my humour. Instead he grasps his cock in his hand, angles it between my legs and growls,

"You want me, don't you? You want me to fuck you hard, don't you?"

"For heaven's sake, baby," I giggle, "you know I do, so would you please just stop tempting me and hurry up because I am desperate to feel you inside me again!"

Raising an eyebrow to me, "You called me baby. That's quite forward at this delicate stage of our relationship, you know!"

I giggle again. Prising my legs apart with his knee, he muses, "Mmm … Tell me my little submissive, how frantic are you for me?"

"So much so that I don't think I can take any more of your games," I quip.

He grins and tells me he has more games up his sleeve and if I play this one to his satisfaction… 'Another game… here in the bath?' then later on, he will introduce me to some new ones… One that he particularly likes that involves a riding crop! He then lets out the most unbelievable sexy chuckle, one that causes shivers to run through my hips and collate at my now-aching centre. Licking his lips, he informs me that because I performed in my first lesson well, he is now going to get me so frustrated that I will be writhing underneath him – and he adds, not only will he have me begging for mercy but he will also have me climbing the walls.

I burst out laughing and quiz, "How on earth do you propose to get me climbing the walls?"

Resting one arm upon the rim of the tub and the other one upon my shoulder, he retreats slightly, and whispers out my name. I breathe his. Within the split of a second, I have no chance to speak, for with such a might of force, as the bath water spills over the curved rim of the tub, he has driven his body hard and deep into mine. All I could do was coil my entire body around him, in the hope of not only holding on but also to keep the driving rhythm that he was pistoning into me from, if it was at all possible, shattering my delicate frame into two halves.

CHAPTER TWENTY-ONE

Sunday Morning

On reaching the bottom step, I smile as I see Darius casually lounging up against the kitchen work surface sipping on his morning coffee. His taut, naked torso is still damp with beads of moisture from his recent shower, and his hair is a ruffled, damp, unruly mess of glorious, thick curls. Taking another sip of the aromatic dark liquid, he places his cup down onto the surface. Hooking his thumbs into the top of his sweatpants, he yanks them down a little and teases, "You like what you see, Helena?"

I laugh and tell him that yes, I like very much what I can see, but how on earth am I going to concentrate on eating my breakfast while trying to abstain from desiring him – could he at least please put on a t-shirt? He chortles away and pushes his sweats just that little bit further down so I can see the soft, downy hair that lies beneath his belly button.

Angling his head to one side and in a sexy drawling tone, he chirps,

"After last night's playtime, are you now hungry for something other than my infamous salmon bagels topped with crème fraiche, my angel?"

I rub my smarting wrists and giggle, "I could be."

"Mmm," he mutters. "I'll think about feeding you with my body in a little while, but for now, this man's tummy's doing a mega rumble, so come, my angel, come and sit with me and let's eat."

Nearly fainting at him calling me his angel, he approaches me and pulls me into his arms. "You're not going to pass out on me, are you, Helena?"

"Well, if you feed me some of that wonderful creation that's sitting on the table over there, then I think I might start to feel better."

He presses his body into me. "Come on; let's eat because I too need some energy. In fact, I need barrels of the stuff because, my precious, after we've eaten, I want to fuck you again until we are both a dripping wet heap of a sweaty mess of hot, scented sex."

Oh.

He then changes tack and I amaze when he asks, "Move in with me, Helena. I need you with me. There is not a damn thing I can do to stop the emotions that are stockpiling in my soul. You make me have a dull ache in my chest... I have never felt that before."

His love flows over me in a crashing, forceful wave.

Wrapping his arms around me, he dips his head low, inhales the scent of my freshly washed hair and again pleas, "Please don't leave me, Helena. I... I..."

I draw back from him, gaze up and when I see the soulful glaze cast in his stunning blue eyes, I feel compelled to hush him with the gentlest of kisses while murmuring to him that I know deep down what he is trying to say. "Are... Are you sure you want me to move in with you? This all seems so unbelievably sudden."

With his heart pounding vividly against my chest, he sighs, "It's not sudden at all. It's... it's… you are all I have thought about since I first set eyes upon you."

With my own heart racing, I say, "If I say yes, how do you propose we should celebrate this most momentous of occasions?"

"Well," he grins, "since it's Sunday and Sundays are designed for being incredibly lazy, I guess I shall have to take you back to my bed, wrap you in my arms and keep you safe."

"Then," I smile, "I do believe, considering that what you have suggested seems like an excellent idea, you now have me, mind, heart, body and soul."

He tips his finger under my chin, angles my face upwards and with a soupçon of shyness in his voice, he whispers, "It was that easy? I have all of you? You'll move in with me?"

I break into a wide smile, brush my lips along his and quietly breathe, "Yes, Darius, it was that easy and yes, you do and I will."

After awakening alone in *our* bed by the scent of freshly brewing coffee that's infusing my nostrils and permeating my senses, I know that Darius, the man I love with my whole heart will not be too far away from me. Using this free moment, I roll over onto his side of the bed and with the goofiest of smiles on my face, I pick up the receiver from the bedside phone and call Angelica.

"Morning, Sweetie."

"Morning, Helena. How are you?"

"Glorious."

"And why may I ask are you feeling so, elated."

"Are you ready for this?"

"Enlighten me," she excitedly asks.

"You'll never guess."

"Probably not, so hurry up and tell me."

"Are you ready to hear my exciting news?"

"Yes. Yes. Yes! Get on with it!"

"I'm… drum roll… moving in with Darius."

"Oh my goodness," she exclaims. "You *are* now a bonafide, film star's girlfriend! I'm soooo green with envy."

We laugh and then I touch on the subject of Darius' brother. "Well firstly, he is soooo adorable."

"And…"

"He's tall, like your hot sex god, but he's not dark and broody, he's blonde, green eyed and the most excellent kisser I have ever come across!"

"Angelica, you never did what I think you did, did you?"

"Let's just say you have so I may have."

Now falling about into fits of hysterical laughter, she then stuns me when she says,

"Imagine if you married Darius and I married Xavier, we'd be sisters-in-law!"

"Now wouldn't that be bizarre?"

"Strange but fun eh?"

I laugh and then say I have to be quick for I think I heard Darius calling me, so I launch into asking her if I may have the week off to pack and move. Without hesitation or question she tells me that of course I can because it's not every day someone she knows is stepping out with a sexy screen god. We both titter away at the latter and then I ask her how she'll cope without me.

"Well as luck would have it my sister, Caren, is over for the week and I know she'll gladly help out!"

"Wonderful, give her my love and I'll pop in during the week and I can fill you in on all the gossip."

"Perfect. I have to go now, Helena, or I'll be late for opening up."

"Okay. Catch you soon, *Sis-in-law*!"

"Bye." She giggles.

"Bye."

Placing the receiver down, I flop back on the bed, take a few blinks, and as the world above me comes into focus, I see the rain droplet, decorated skylight suspended above me. I warmly smile to myself. *This is a slice of luxurious heaven.* Stepping out of bed, I grasp my gown from the floor, wrap it around me, and pad out of the room. Following the scent of the enticing dark, aromatic beans, I soon find myself standing outside the kitchen. Leaning up against the architrave, I drink in the manly vision before me. Darius is draped upon the bar stool. His long legs are crossed and he is turning a page of this morning's newspaper. While he pushes his reading glasses up the bridge of his nose, he elegantly sips upon a cup of coffee; I can't take my eyes off the sensuous curve of his bowed lips as they rest upon the china rim. Forcing myself to stop ogling his mouth, I turn my attention to his dark, silken locks. His hair is immaculately styled and right now, this very minute, I would give anything to tousle his pristine curls into a heap of a tangled mess.

I melt even further when I assess his attire. He is wearing a navy-blue pinstripe well-tailored suit, which is complimented by a light blue, French cuffed shirt and a darker shade of an azure blue tie. My vision travels down his legs and I halt when I reach his feet. They are graced with a pair of shiny dark blue oxfords. He looks so elegant, so graceful.

Glancing up from his read, he sees me, removes his reading glasses and settles the newspaper down onto the breakfast bar. Resting an elbow on the table top, he beams,

"Good Morning, my precious. I trust you slept well?"

"Good morning, Mr Carter!" I giggle. "I slept very, very well indeed!"

With his chin resting upon his curled up fist, he tells me that I don't have to address him by his title as we are not in D/s mode. I respond by saying that I wished we were. He looks startled at hearing the latter and rises from his seat. Striding towards me, on reaching me, he cups my face in his hands, looks deep and lovingly at me and breathes, "I wish we were too but unfortunately, my precious, I have to go to work."

"Could we, you know," I blush, "Could we have a quickie before you go?"

He draws my face up to him, presses his lips to mine and while the fresh linen laundered scent of him and the hedonistic cocktail of Chanel Bleu and his pheromones invades and enraptures my senses, I quiver inside when he in explicit detail softly whispers, "I would love nothing more that bend you over the breakfast bar, pull your panties to one side – assuming you are wearing a pair and sink my cock deep between the folds of your luscious body, but alas," he sighs, "I'm already late enough as it is, so I will have to take a rain-check on that for later."

I give him a playful swat and ask "Are you sure?"

Skimming my lips with his, he murmurs, "Not sure, but my darling I really have to go right now. I have to be on set in an hour."

"Since I have taken the week off work to get-to-know-you, can I come with you? I'd love to see you performing on set."

He draws back from me, and creases an extremely deep, concerned frown. "No, Helena. I never want you to see… see…" he pauses and then presses his finger to my lips. "Hush, precious," he silences and then stuns me when he divulges, "now, listen to me. In my study, I know you'll poke around the condo and find the room, on my desk you will find an American Express gold credit card. It's for you. It's yours.

There is no limits on what you are allowed to spend, just don't go mad and buy a yacht or anything too pricy on your first visit out." He then winks at me, chuckles and resumes, "Giorgio will be at your disposal whenever you wish. He will drive you anywhere you wish to go. Spend the day shopping, lunching with Angelica, or anything you want to do, but do me one favour, while you're out, buy yourself some sexy lingerie. I think something lacy, black and alluring would be beautiful on you," and he then sheepishly adds, "I want to make love to you while you are wearing it tonight."

Before I can answer, he removes his finger from my lips, cups the back of my head in his hand. Tilting his head to one side, he tells me how much he adores me and that next to the card I will find a new phone. He informs me that he had purchased me the latest one because I must keep up with evolving technology and that it also contains all the varying contact numbers of his – *he will always be within my reach. It also has Giorgio's call number.*

"Darius," I amaze. "That's way too generous. I can't possibly accept either of these gifts."

Placing his hands on either side of my shoulders, he looks deep into my eyes and says, "You can and you will, Helena. I need to know that firstly you can always contact me and secondly, I *want* to spoil you. I want you to want for nothing."

"But… But…" I protest.

"There are no buts, Helena. For once," he sighs, "just don't fight against me, please because I do find it rather exhausting."

"Okay," I agree. "But I want you to know that I am overwhelmed by your generosity."

He kisses me lightly on the tip of my nose while responding that he understands and while he lingers a little longer than I expected, I find myself asking, "Do you know who Angelica's dating?"

With a touch of certainty in his voice, he whispers, "Tell me, baby, who is the lucky man that's snared your boss?"

"Your brother, Xavier."

Drawing back from me, he winks at me, and tells me that he loves it when a plan comes together and that truly he has to go now.

"Will you tell me more about Xavier tonight over dinner?"

Walking away from me he says, "If that is what you wish, Helena."

While he collates his keys and briefcase, I blurt, "Is he a secret dominant too, like you?"

Snapping upright, he frowns, and then flippantly replies, "I wouldn't know, Helena. If he is, then firstly it is none of my business and secondly a man's private life is just that – *private.*"

Feeling a little embarrassed at latter my question and his following answer, I tentatively say, "Oh… I guess you may be right."

"There's no guessing about it," he dismisses. "On this matter, I *am* right."

Before I get a chance to even agree with him, he's already heading backwards out of the doorway whilst blowing me a kiss.

CHAPTER TWENTY-TWO

SELFRIDGES

As Giorgio holds the car door open for me, he extends his arm to me and I offer him my hand. Drawing me to me feet, I speak, "Thank you, Giorgio."
He gives me a fatherly smile and replies, "You're welcome, Helena. Just call me when you would like me to collect you."
"I will. Bye for now."
"Goodbye, Ms Helena."

Standing here on the pavement, I look up at the building before me. Seeing the name 'Selfridges' scribed across the front, a mixture of excitement and anticipation floods over me. I have only ever dreamt about being inside this store, and I never imagined in my entire life that I would now be setting foot inside this most famous of retails establishments.

THE LINGERIE DEPARTMENT

Holding up a thin, black coloured flimsy G-string, I wonder as to how much it costs. Fingering the tag, I have to catch my breath when I see that it costs a whopping whole £375.00. Aghast at the price, I exclaim out, "Never in a million years can that price be correct!" I then quietly muse, "It could so easily be ripped to shreds in seconds by a firmish tug of Darius' hand." As I am about to place the almost non-existent string of underwear back onto the rail, I feel a presence ominously close behind me. While the familiar linen perfume of a freshly bathed, alpha male combines with the top notes of arousing cologne, both enrapture my senses. As the hairs on the nape of my neck instantly stand to attention, I still. Wanting, *needing* to turn around to see if I am correct in my assumption as to who exactly is behind me, the second I decide to, I am halted because my ponytail is now being swept to one side in a familiar manner, and this mystery person's fingers are fleeting against the hollow that lies at the base of my neck. While an arm snakes around my waist and holds me firm, I bow my head to see a pristine light-blue, French cuff peeking out from the hem of a pinstripe blue suit. As a hand settles upon my midriff, fingers drum against my belly, and I melt when I hear the owner of the said arm seductively suggest, "If you'd like to go and try that pretty piece of lingerie on for me, Helena, I could show you how easily I could remove it from your person."

I giggle at this male's cheekiness, push my rear into him and ask, "What on earth are you doing here, Darius? I thought you had a busy schedule ahead of you today?"

Nuzzling in to me, he kisses me on my cheek and replies, "I got bored of acting, well pretending, so I thought I'd enlighten my laborious day by spying on you."

I laugh and express, "You're crazy, Darius."

Now cradling me, his manhood stiffening against my buttocks, he sexily whispers, "Be an angel for me and go and try it on."

"You wish me to try it on right this very minute?" I exclaim.

"Correct," he affirms.

I oblige his ask.

THE CUBICLE

While I am admiring my semi-clad reflection in the full length mirror, I hear the lock to the dressing room click shut. The encapsulating sound causes me to avert my gaze from my semi-naked person and I see Darius projected behind me. He's slowly walking towards me. His suit jacket is draped precariously over his shoulders. Shrugging it off, he catches it in his hand and tosses onto the chair situated in the corner of this lavish room. I shudder because he is now unbuckling his leather belt. On hearing it whoosh free from the loops of his waistband, I again tremble with anticipation.

Am I in for another one of Darius' possible ten strikes of a lashing? Surely he would do that act here in Selfridges, where my sounds of eroticism would be heard tenfold! And certainly not with that belt!

Placing hands on the back of my head, I decide that I will release my hair from the band that secures my ponytail, *I think he would like to see my hair flow down my back*. As my fingers locate the violet coloured elastic, I hear him hush for me to leave it in place.

With his presence now filling the room, he orders, "Turn around for I want to see how much you desire me."

I turn and he leans in close and breathes against my lips, "After I've finished consuming you, you will never need reminding of whom you belong to, Helena. Do you understand what I mean?"

I do.

Pressing his forehead to mine, he asks me to turn and lay my front down onto the table. My bare breasts are now flush with the frosted glass table top, and the coolness of the surface chills my skin causing my nipples to stiffen. While I dangerously teeter upon a pair of gold Jimmy Choo heels that were left, I assume, for me in the cubicle, I widen my legs in expectation for his first touch, and I quake inside when I hear the dulcet tones of his voice sift through the magnolia scented air. Making no hesitation in delaying the inevitable any longer, he presses his palms flush either side of my head and aligns his body with mine, sensually whispering into my ear, "You're more than magnificent, Helena. You're an astounding brunette of a beauty. And knowing that I can have you any place, any time I wish makes me a very replete dominant."

Ditto, Darius! And it also makes me a very replete submissive.

While his fresh manly scent envelopes me, with his finger, he agonisingly slowly trails it up my inner left thigh, and I arouse further when he so, so lowly purrs, "I can't wait to flick that flimsy expensive string of yours to one side and sink my cock deep into that plush, tight pussy of yours."

On hearing his erotic, suggestive phrase – a heavenly 'O' escapes from between my parted lips – and within a breath, his fingers have deftly located the band of the string that is gracing my midriff. I flex a tad on my heels as he holds said band firm in fist and upwardly tugs it against my folds. While he doesn't release his grasp on the delicate silk, a small pleasing moan escapes from my lips and he amusingly enquires, "Am I turning you on, Helena?"

Oh yes! Very much so, Mr Carter! Keep going!

I mewl out a yes and he replays his actions. The peachy-coloured fabric is caressing my swelling nub, and as I revel in this most risky, yet hedonistically divine of pleasurable sensations, he, in a low, throaty rumble barrages me with a series of rather sexually provoking questions.

"Am I making that perfect, plush, pussy of yours throb like crazy? Are you craving to feel my cock filling you? Do you want me to put a little pressure your clitoris with my saliva coated fingertip while I take your body onto another plane?"

Jeez, Darius! That's some choice of descriptive words! And I silently affirm a yes to all your questions!

The sound of a rash unzipping of trousers, causes my thighs to tremble. *This is it! Take a deep breath, Helena.* With his front now flush with my back, he slowly aligns his body with mine. I draw a large gulp of air and he settles into position.

"I want you, Mr Carter," I declare and include, "I am desperately aching to feel you inside me."

He responds to me by firstly chuckling that he likes the fact that I am calling him Mr Carter and that for my display of good manners he will reward me later!

How exciting! A reward? A gold sticker star perhaps, I giggle to myself... If so, how very, very gracious of him!

Secondly, he shoves his knee between my legs, spreads my legs a little more and declares, "Trust me when I tell you this; you are going to have me any moment now and I promise you, you will never, ever forget a single, erotic second of it!"

While his hand comes around to my jaw, he tenderly clamps his hand over my mouth, whilst informing me that the reason why he is choosing to perform this action on me is to prevent my cries of passion being heard by the assistants and shoppers who are buzzing around on other side of this plush, spacious cubicle door. With the thought of the general public on the other side of the door, heightening my sexuality even more, I draw in a breath only to have the air stripped from my lungs when he indeed does give himself to me in the most carnal fashion I have ever experienced.

The flimsy string was dragged to one side, and as he sank his manhood deep into my quivering centre, my muscles countered by clenching and spasming over his thick, veined cock. With each powerful upward thrust of him, my muffled whimpers multiplied and intensified in their intensity. My breath heaved against the warmth of his palm, and as he ground deeper and deeper into me, on what I assumed must be the final, frantic grind of his hips battering against my body, I sank my teeth into the dampening flesh of his hand. Biting him hard again, I sucked on his puncture wound tasting a smattering of his blood. He rasped out my name in such a fashion that I couldn't prevent myself from repeating my actions. As he removed his hand from my mouth, he hissed into my ear, "Ow, you little bitch! That damn well hurt!"

"Good!" I venomously responded. "You deserved a nip for your fieriness, you horny bastard!"

"That was no fucking dainty nip you feisty little mare," he grumbled. "It was more of a tear-of-flesh and since you were bold enough to draw and taste my blood, I'm now am going to rip your underwear from your person!"

'O'… 'O'… 'O'.

"And," he gruffed and emphasised, "you are going to enjoy the sensation as it tears against your wet, swollen flesh. I'm estimating after the pounding that I will have just given you that you will be feeling rather tender between those quivering thighs of yours, yes?"

Quadruple 'O', Mr Carter! And yes my flesh is most definitely smarting, sir!

I outwardly groaned at his descriptive words, and I most definitely wailed out a little too loud, because with one final, core hitting propulsion of his cock into me, my muscles contracted, and while they responded by rapidly milking him,

I felt every precious drop of his hot, pearlesque fluid splatter against the walls of my aching centre. He then snaked an arm around my waist, and hovered me above the table top. His cock continued pulsating inside me, and through an abundance of his short, sharp breaths, he kissed me gently on the roundness of my left shoulder. Soothing to me just how perfect I am, I became lost within the delicacy, the tenderness of the love he was showing to me, and just as my breath also began to labour, he propelled me into another dimension by indeed taking me by surprise and ripping said string from my person. He then ended our risqué adventure in Selfridges by slapping me extremely hard on my arse and declaring that we should now get cleaned up, dressed and go our separate ways.

How matter-of-fact, sterile or practical?

I dragged my body up, turned to face him and when I saw him stuffing the shredded string into his trouser pocket, I gasped to him what are we to do? We hadn't paid for it and we most certainly couldn't return it in the sad, limp condition it was now in! With a devious chuckle falling from his lips, he admitted to me that he had purchased it earlier on and that as it now was his property, he was more than satisfied!

CHAPTER TWENTY-THREE

Connor O'Denbiegh

With my head bowed down, I hurriedly race through the foyer of the store. I desperately need to be outside in the fresh air, because I'm feeling so breathless after Darius' surprise *performance* within the confines of the changing cubicle. *I'm seriously beginning to question as to whether I can keep up with this rather insatiable sexual appetite of his.* On making it outside, I don't see the world passing me by, I just lean up against the wall, close my eyes and suck as much air as I possibly can into my lungs. While the oxygen fills my person and starts to revitalise me, from out of the blue, I hear a familiar voice from my past question, "Helena? Helena? Is that you?"

Flicking my lashes open, I go into a state of undeniable disbelief when I see my first ever love, Connor O'Denbiegh, standing right before my very eyes. Doing a double take, I find my voice and in a surprised tone, I reply, "Good grief! If it isn't the young boy that used to chase me around his family's apple orchards standing right before me!"

"Blimey, Helena!" he amuses and reflects. "If it isn't you all grown up and still as beautiful as ever standing right before me."

A few seconds pass and we both fall about in a series of childish giggles. As he sweeps his messy fringe from his eyes, he beams me an infectious smile and I ask, "What are you doing here in England, Connor? The last I heard from your sister was that you were on your way to Australia to fulfil your dream to become a world famous wind surfer."

"I was, Helena." He drops his lashes and in a saddened voice, he adds, "It's a very, very long and complicated story."

Oh what happened to my dear, sweet, Connor? I wonder.

With my curiosity now stirred and the memories of my first kiss among other romantic interludes that I experienced with him warming my heart, I suggest, "How about we go for a coffee and then you can tell me all about your wonderful adventure."

Immediately he raises his look, breaks into a memorable boyish grin and tells me that he knows a cute little barista bar not too far away from here.

"Great!" I whoop. "Show me the way, my long-lost bestie!"

Offering me his arm, I link in with him and he leads us forth. As we walk, neither of us speaks. Sometimes I guess at particular moments in time like these, that there is no need for any words to be exchanged.

CHAPTER TWENTY-FOUR

Swirling the froth on the top of my cappuccino with a teaspoon, I then place it to my lips and while I taste the milky flavour, I transfix upon Connor. His blonde hair is a sun-bleached mop of an unruly mess *much like a facet of his personality back in the day* all the little freckles that are peppered on his ski slope of a nose are more prominent that usual and I'm guessing this is because of the time he has spent lazing around in the scorching Australian sun. While I gaze into his almond-shaped, green eyes, searching for something to give me a clue as to why he is feeling so downcast, he places his cup to his lips, takes a sip, bats his curly, blonde lashes at me, and as they flitter and flutter, with that motion of his alone, I feel a dangerous rekindling of a love-once-lost spark within me.

This is extremely dangerous territory, Helena. Remember you are Darius' girlfriend now.

"So, Helena," he half smiles. "What have you been up to since we parted? Did you make it into the wonderful world of glamour modelling?"

I pop the spoon back in the creamy liquid, stir my coffee and muse as to if I should tell him about Darius. I quickly decide not to for what would be the point right now?

"Not as yet." I say. "I'm kind of still working on my portfolio and I am now working full time in a florist's shop."

Raising his eyebrows, he says, "Florists eh? Nice."

"It is. I enjoy being surrounded by flowers and I have a very nice boss called Angelica."

"Mmm, how nice?" he chuckles. "Nice enough for me to date?"

I frown. *You're not going anywhere near her, Connor!*

"So, you're still perfecting your portfolio? It's been four years and you're still not satisfied with the photographs taken of you?"

I shake my head from side to side as to signal a no.

"Shame," he adds, "I always thought the ones I took of you were rather alluring."

I blush, remembering our teenage years - *The photo-shoot in the autumn – me semi-naked laying on the morning, dewy grass, surrounded by an abundance of golden fallen leaves and red shiny apples.*

"Lately I've been thinking that if I was really that passionate about modelling, I would've nailed it by now, but I guess, with hindsight, it's probably not really what I wish to do now."

"Oh damn," he says. "I was looking forward to opening up a lad's mag and seeing you as Miss January lying naked on a snowy log with a few scattered pieces of holly strategically placed upon your person!"

I laugh out at his cheekiness because he knows full well, that I wouldn't do *that* sort of modelling! With a little tease in my voice, I prompt, "So, Connor, tell me all about your adventure in Oz. I'm guessing there were plenty of wild parties, plenty of sex on the beach with hot Australian blonde girls eh?"

He reclines back into his chair, and places his hands behind his head. While an unfathomable look spreads across his face, he in a casual, laid back tone, flouts, "I can assure you there *was* an abundance of drunken celebrations, in which I performed magnificently in and thoroughly enjoyed to full!"

"Oh," surprised "Care to tell me more!"

"And guess what else I took immense pleasure in my beautiful, alluring, Helena?"

Now feeling deadly curious, I quiz, "What else did you rejoice in?"

He slowly leans over the table, takes my hands in his, and tilts his head to one side. Raising an eyebrow, the corners of his lips turn up and he breaks into a mischievous smile. I reflect a smile back at him, only for it to quickly disappear when he stupefies me with the following words. "During every single one of the parties, I made sure I succeeded in banging my way through many a willing and drop dead gorgeous bird! Sometimes I'd pleasure two or three on a good night. Sometimes, if the aphrodisiacs kicked in on time, I'd make out with two hot lovelies at a time – three, if last two beauties hadn't managed to drain me!"

Wholly shocked at his declaration and intensely horrified at how he has become to view woman as nothing more than mere sex objects, I snatch my hands back away from him, and muse as to why this once gentle, sweet man has become so self-centred. A few strained moments pass and my iPhone pings to signal an incoming message – *Darius* – As the shrill sound snaps me back into some sort of reality, I look over at Connor, whose complexion is now pale as can be and I ask, "What on earth has happened to you? When and why did you my sweet, dear friend, manifest into this rampant sex monster?"

He pushes his cup to one side, leans forward. His breath is now as close to my ear as can be, and as he stutters,

"When I realised that I... I... still... still..."

We are interrupted from conversing any further when my phone signals to me again that I have another message –Darius

– it is rapidly followed by another shuddering ping! Connor quickly retreats from me, reclines back into his seat and once again places his hands behind his head, but this time he doesn't look at me, instead he rocks back on his chair and stares vacantly up at the ceiling.

Pulling out my phone, I see that there are three unread messages from Darius. This is how the conversation unravelled:

Message one: Where are you baby?

Message two: Where are you, Helena?

Message three: Where the fuck are you, Helena?

Why?

Are you still spending my money?

Nope. Your bank account is still lucrative. I'm having coffee with an old friend.

Is this so-called friend a male or a female?

Oh he's most definitely a male.

Male?

Yup! A fully red-blooded alpha male! – Just like you!

There's no one quite like me! I can assure you of that!

I concur.

You're making me cross with your unnecessary teasing, Helena. I should punish you, you know!

Good and great! Another one of your legendary spankings in the offering! How yawnful!

Don't be such a sarcastic mare! You're going to receive more than a pair of red, sore buttocks when I've finished reminding you who you belong to.

Yes, O bossy one! And may I ask with what you are going to chastise me with?

Its untexable what I am going to penalise you with!

Oh – Giggling here, Mr Carter!

Not tittering here in the slightest, my feisty little submissive. Now, where are you? I'm coming to get you.

Don't be so silly. I'll be done soon. Love you, and looking forward to your earlier gesture of a reward plus latest suggested reprimand! Bye!

I shove my phone back into my pocket only to miss the latest message which later when I did read, I cried pitifully. This is the admittance from Darius:

You said you love me, Helena?

I love you too.

I love you.

I love you.

By god, do I love you like no other!

Helena, stay put because I promise you I will be with you soon.

Now feeling a tad triumphant at not letting Darius control me, I turn my attention back to Connor. He's now looking directly at me. His eyes are brimming with a saddened look and I don't want to leave him like this so I ask,

"Hey, Connor, you look a little pale, are you feeling all right?"

He half-smiles, tells me that his tummy's rumbling – *he's always hungry if I remember rightly* – and then asks, "Who was that texting you?"

"My boyfriend. He was just wondering when I would be home."

In a surprised tone, he exclaims, "Oh, you have a lover?"

"Yes, I do and I better go and see him."

Next, from out of the blue, he asks, "Do you love him?"

I fumble with the paper napkin next to my cup and not wanting to admit out loud that I do love Darius, I say that I think I do.

"Don't you know whether you love him or not?"

"Well it's early days in our relationship. I guess only time will tell."

"How long have you been seeing him?"

"Just a short while... Not long really at all."

Noisily draining his cup of its contents, he smacks his lips together and sticks out his bottom lip. "Okay. I suppose I understand about that but do you have to go back to him right now, Ellie."

My head now spinning at hearing Connor call me by the pet name – *Ellie* – he christened me with on the afternoon we lost our virginities to each other I squeak, "No, not at all, so why don't we up sticks and go and find somewhere to eat?"

"So you still want to talk with me. I haven't turned you away from me because of what I said about my past rampant sex life?"

"Of course I want to talk with you. You're my dearest friend. Whatever you've done between the grains of sand is not for me to judge. We all have private lives. I just want to know everything that has happened to you."

With his eyes now dancing with a million questions at the latter, he blows a light puff of air upwards and breathes, "Thank you, Ellie. I knew you of all people would understand me."

Warmly smiling at him, I add, "But there is one thing I need to understand before we move on."

"Anything... You can ask me anything you wish and I will answer you truthfully."

"Why did you leave Oz?"

Without blinking, he looks at me stark and reveals that the reason he left was because for the last year, he had been having a rather torrid affair with the senator's wife. *She, Maria, was a good ten years older than Connor, but age when you're in love is no matter… No matter at all.* One night, Senator Bradley Harvey came home early, which for him was highly out of character, and caught them to put it bluntly, fucking in the summerhouse. The crux of the matter was that she was torn from Connor and he was given an ultimatum – to either return to his homeland or to face the twisted wrath that goes with the spin of a politician's hand. He chose to up sticks and flee home.

"So, there you have it, Ellie. I'm in a bit of a pickly mess. In fact," he sighs and murmurs, "I'm in a right royal mess."

Suddenly I feel so forlorn for him, so I grasp his hand in mine and squeeze it tight. "Did you… you… love her?" I quietly ask.

He runs his finger along his bottom lip and moves me deep when he replies, "Yes. Well I *sort* of loved her." He pauses and then softly speaks. "I know she loved me."

"If you sort of loved her, why didn't you fight to keep her? Why didn't you ask her to divorce her husband?"

"She did want me to fight for her. I wanted to *save* her, Ellie, truly I did but after a heated and rather lengthy discussion we both came to the conclusion that it would be to no avail. He wouldn't let her divorce him anyway."

"Why wouldn't he let her go?"

"Because, Bradley Harvey *is* a fucking self-centred control freak, Helena." He rasps. "You know the type well, remember?"

I have to admit that even thought I don't wish to remember, I do – as my own horrific memories of my parent's torrid marriage fleets through my mind, the flamboyant antics, and the controlling way that my father put upon my mother springs to my mind.

"He doesn't love her, he never did," he shudders, bravely continues and as his shoulders slump, his head droops into his chest. "He just married her because she came from a well-to-do-family. He just doesn't want anyone else to have her so her life is a farce, a false pretence and damn right sad."

"What did her husband threaten you with?"

As I hear the words – *murder* – fall from his lips, I have to choke back a forthcoming sob.

Rising from my seat, I guide him up and suggest we now go and find a place to eat. He doesn't answer me; he just shuffles along in his battered converse sneakers and lets me lead him out into the early evening's air.

THE TAPAS BAR

Picking up a mini mouth-watering manchego ham tapas from the turntable, I place it to my lips. As I go to take a bite, the delectable creation never has a chance to settle upon my tongue. The reason for this is, as I panned around the restaurant, I spotted a very dark and moody Darius striding towards us. Now feeling confused as to how he had found me, my fingers trembled and as the tempting morsel fell from my digits, it clumsily plopped back onto the plate. With a mouthful of food being noisily grinded between his perfectly straight white teeth, Connor muffles, "What's up, Ellie? You look like you've seen a ghost!"

"Oh that's no ghost I spot," I murmur,

"Well if it ain't a ghost," he mumbles, "Who is it?"

Trying to sound *nonchalant,* I reply, "Erm… It's just my cross-looking boyfriend strutting towards us."

"O—O—" he gingerly responds. "Is my autumn-queen going to be in a shit load of trouble?"

"I don't know." I shrug.

Spanking alert!

"Well if she is then I, 'Connor-Lord-of-the-apple-orchard-and-protector-of-said-queen' will arm oneself with a sling and pelt cross-looking-boyfriend with a cache of maggoty-rotten apples until he retreats back to the undergrowth from whence he came!"

In between my giggles, the mere thought of pristine Darius coated in the pulp and juice of decomposing red russets fuels my titters even further, and when I finally manage to calm down, I plead endlessly with Connor to stop making me laugh. He winks, shrugs his shoulders as if to say if you wish me to stop, I will stop and also I'm sorry. He then continues stuffing his face with more nibbles, and I focus upon my *grumpy dominant* that is almost upon me.

On reaching me, he stands directly behind me, places his hand upon my shoulder and with a hint of sharpness in his voice hisses into my ear, "So, Helena, is this the old friend you were telling me about?"

I nod and his grip tightens. He then steps aside, extends his arm to Connor and offers him his hand. Connor, - the mannerless – doesn't look up from his plate of food; he just swipes his hand until it makes contact with Darius'. As I watch both men momentarily curl their fingers around each other's, their knuckles whitening, my tummy flips. During that briefest of handshakes, Darius declares his title. Connor, on the other hand, doesn't offer his name, he just shamelessly blurts out loud, "Screwing a movie star, Ellie? You never said! I must say my enchanting-Queen-of-the-apple-orchard that's bonza!"

In retort to his words, Darius distastefully snorts, and then orders rather than suggests that it is time for us to leave. I'm exhausted by today's events, so I, without hesitation rise from my seat.

"Bye, Connor." I delicately say. "It was so lovely to see you again."

He doesn't look up from the table. It's almost as if he does not want to acknowledge the fact that I have to go.

What Darius did next completely threw me. Snaking his hand around the back of my neck, he drew me into him, and while nipping the lobe of my ear, he hissed, "*My enchanting-Queen-of-the-apple-orchard*. What the fuck's that all about?" He then chills me to the very inner core when he growls – *and Ellie?"*

I tremble at the annoyance in his voice and I quell even further when he sarcastically rasps, "When I get you home-enchanting-Queen-of-the-apple-orchard I am going to teach you a very important lesson and afterwards, I can assure you, you will never go absent-without-leave on me again! Do you understand me, Helena?"

Yeah, I understand you, you miserable, control freaking git! We will see how tonight pans out!

I shrug my shoulders and now wishing that I could stay and talk with Connor some more, I subtly shove Darius away from me, regain my composure and head towards the checkout. He doesn't appear by my side, thankfully. I think he has sensed that I am on the brink of one of my feisty outbursts. After settling the bill, I surreptitiously write my cell number down on a napkin, hand it to the waitress and ask her to give it to Connor after I have left.

She smiles and agrees.

I leave her a handsome tip.

CHAPTER TWENTY-FIVE

As Darius presses his foot flush to the accelerator and the Porsche fires into motion, I am propelled flush against the back of the passenger seat. Slightly startled at the impact of my body slamming against the grey, sumptuous leather, I regain my composure and glance over at him. I see that his hands are gripping the steering wheel so firm that under that pressurizing hold of his, his knuckles have whitened. My vision then travels to his facial profile. He appears to be clenching his teeth together and I guess my assumption must be correct for I am noticing a muscle spasming continually under the stubbly, midnight shadow that's highlighting his strong jawbone. We continue motoring in a strained silence only to halt when we approach a set of red traffic lights. He's now drumming his fingers on the wheel in such an irritating fashion that I decide I am going to ask him to stop doing that annoyance.

As I go to speak, his voice snaps through the snug confined space of the car and it spits at me, "Did he fuck you?"

The lights have now changed to amber and he's repetitively growling under his breath, "He did, didn't he? The seedy little fucker! If he has, I'll murder the bastard with my bare hands if he touched a single centimetre of your body!"

Not wishing to speak with him, I stare out of the window wishing that I could reverse time and be with Connor in the apple orchard the moments before we lost our innocence.

Amber has now given way to green and with Darius' question still unanswered, we accelerate off again. A matter of moments pass and I am taken by surprise when he eases off the gas, indicates left and the car careers in said direction. As the tyres wail a deafening screech, the motor swerves into a well-lit underground car park, and it begins to slow down.

With my vision now focused straight ahead, I see a parking space coming into view. The vehicle is rolled into it, the engine is switched off and the handbrake is applied. With us now stationary, he unbuckles both our belts and then, in such a blunt tone, orders me to get out of the car.

Feeling utterly phased by this situation, I open the door, if for anything to be away from him. Before my feet can even touch the tarmac, I look up and see him standing before me. In a split of a second, my forearm is grasped and I am hauled like a heavy sack of spuds out of the car. Slamming the door shut behind me, he shoves me up against the car and his grip on me tightens. With my left shoulder now beginning to ache, I cry out, "What the fuck are you doing, Darius? Let go of me, you're hurting me!"

He quickly releases me and while his brooding stare bores through to my very soul, he sneers, "Hush that filthy mouth of yours, Helena! I've warned you before about swearing at me!"

I groan out and he snakes his hand around the back of my neck. His touch is now bordering on electrifying. Entangling his fingers in my tresses, he lightly tugs at my locks and in a slightly calmer tone, he asks me again if Connor had touched me. I'm so exhausted by this whole day, this scenario here that I don't even think about what may transpire from my answer and a *yes* falls from my lips.

His spine immediately stiffens and I am released from his hold in such a way one would've thought that I was a tarantula who had just stung her prey with a deadly, black poison. He's now gingerly stepping back from me and running his fingers through his silken dark curls. A look of stark shock is plastered across his handsome face and I can't hold his attention any longer so I avert my gaze from him and direct it at the floor beneath my feet. A few moments pass and he jolts me back to into this insane reality with a one worded question. "When?"

Still looking at the floor, I stammer, "When what?"

"When did you let that bleach-blonde, bastard fuck you?"

I raise my lashes, meet his icy stare and defend. "He's not a bastard. His parents are married."

With his fists now knotted at his sides, he rasps, "Very droll indeed Helena... Now enough of the technicalities and tell me when did he fuck you?"

Desperately wanting to quash this scenario, I quickly answer, "When... I... I... Was..."

His voice now straining, he demands, "When exactly, Helena? Was it this afternoon, soon after we'd had our little session in Selfridges? Where did you do it? Was it in some urine stinking alleyway with your back flush up against the cold brick wall? You like being wall banged? Or was it on a single bed at some cheap knock off hotel?"

With the tears now forming in the back of my eyes, I try so hard to hold back a sob for I just can't believe that he would even think I would let another man touch me. *After all, I have told him I love him, even if it was by a mere text message.* While my tears freely fall, he crushes my soul even further, by leaning into me, tipping his finger under my chin and angling my face upwards. Glaring at me, he wipes away a lone salty globule of emotion from my cheek, places the pad of his finger to my lower lip and rests it there.

"Crocodile tears, Helena?" he harshly grates. "Is *my* queen acting a little drama all of her very own?"

No... No... No... These are my truest heartfelt emotions, Darius. If only you knew.

With his touch alone, my heart begins to splinter and it fragments even more when he quips the following, "Well since you won't answer my question, try digesting these ones. Are you a closet, nymphomaniac whore? Couldn't my cock satisfy you for a few hours at least? Do you get some kick out of being fucked by one man followed by another in the same day?"

My head now in a total spin at the dire vulgarity of his words, I slump against the car and without any forewarning, my legs buckle. I'm now kneeling at his feet, and as my tears halt, I find myself answering to his navy blue, shiny oxfords.

"I am not a nymphomaniac whore." Gasping for air, I hiccup and soulfully cry, "I... I am a one-woman man." I draw another much needed blast of air and with a hint of sarcasm wavering in my voice, I answer, "Yes, your *perfect* manhood did satisfy me and I can assure you, Darius, that it always will."

As his feet shuffle before me, I then swallow and honestly declare my final reply. "Connor was the man whom I lost my virginity to when I was sixteen years old. That was the one and only time we ever... we ever," I sob, "We ever made love. It was coarse, rushed and... and..."

Finishing my sentence, he callously adds, "Foolish?"

"No... How can you say such hurtful a thing? You were a virgin once."

I hear him mumble *Oh fuck it* under his breath followed by him cursing to himself that he is an idiot.

Right now, yes you are Darius!

His voice gentle, I hear him say, "It's all right, Helena."

But I don't look up to him, I just continue. "It... It wasn't a mindless joining of bodies and souls... It... it... was..."

I take the deepest of breaths that I possibly can and as the word... *Love* leaves my soul; his oxfords now disappear from my view. I can't choke any more words so I take a secret look upwards to see him stooping down to meet me. Without passing any further judgment on me, he then scoops me up in his arms and my body goes limp. On hearing the lock of the car turn, he cradles and carries me like I am some sort of precious cargo in the direction of what, through my fogged-out tears, I assume to be the elevator that leads to somewhere only he knows.

CHAPTER TWENTY-SIX

DARIUS

Helena is a forceful, magnetic addiction – Over time, she has become my daily narcotic-free drug and when I finally breathe, admit to her, that I love her, it will not be because we are sexually compatible, it will be because she has and always will be able to leave me breathless by her presence alone.

Aligning his body with mine, once again, Darius transfixes his enchanting gaze upon me and by that look alone, he knows he's already left me wanting. While his steely-blue irises glimmer with a sublime, dewy, lustful mist, he slowly trails his warm fingers down my sides. On reaching my hips, he momentarily pauses, slides his hands under my buttocks, and I reciprocate by angling my hips up towards him. He's now cradling my cheeks in his palms, and as I breathe out, he breaks into one of the most delightful smiles I have ever seen. With such tenderness, he lifts me into him and I'm held firm. Relishing in the hedonistic sensation of his cock filling me, while his manhood throbs away between my moistening folds, he lets out a low-throaty rumble and nuzzles his cheek into the crook of my neck. The warmth of his persona is now enveloping and enrapturing me, and I feel as if it won't be long before he has aided me in elevating onto another undiscovered, sexual plateau. On hearing him say, "Helena, I'm now going to show you why you will never want another man to touch you."

My heart does something mysterious of its own. He's now starting to set a timely rhythm, and with each gentle stroke of his hardness encouraging a series of small contractual waves to accumulate and multiply at my hips, I hush out his name and quietly ask, "And how are you going to do that?"

Stilling, he creases his brow, narrows his gaze, and without a trace of hesitation in his voice, he launches in a speech that leaves me breathless.

"Like this, my precious; with each kiss that I am about to bestow upon you, there will be a thousand reasons hidden in each one of them that will ensure that you will never desire to belong to anyone else but me. While I turn your svelte body over, and I linger my fingertips from the nape of your neck, slowly tracing them down the centre of your spine, I will in fact be charting the typography of your being. I will be noting every mark of birth that is imprinted upon your flesh. And over time, I will leave my own intricate imprints upon your sweat-soaked, sex-drenched, heated skin. As I claim you from behind, and while I take enjoyment from hearing the erotic sounds that fall from your lips, I will not only be extremely close to the sweetest of releases, but once again, I will also have become so lost within you that for me there will never be another. When you finally manage to find your voice and chant out the syllables of my name, I will still while your orgasm shreds you to tatters and ripples over me. As your muscles milk my pearlesque fluid, temporarily draining me for the moment, it will be then, as our breathings slowly return to normal, that we realise that we have now evolved in a whole.

He's now straddling me from behind, and as each one of his successive light, peppery kisses make contact with the curvature of my spine, and just as he reaches the sensitive spot at the nape of my neck, he momentarily pauses. A spine-tingling, lowly moan escapes from his lips, and I quiver inside with a strange concoction of anticipation and excitement. Now continuing his teasing onslaught, he winds my plaited, red tresses around his hand. Gripping tight onto my ponytail tight, in a firm, dominant manner, he jars my head backwards and then in a low-throaty and extremely deeply sexual tone, he quivers me to the bone when he growls into my ear, "Is this what you secretly desire, Helena. Not being in control of your svelte body?"

I have to admit that being submissive to him does something arousing to me and while I feel his arm snake under my belly, he nips me hard on the brink of my shoulder and yanks me onto all fours. I let out a yelp and like a boa constrictor about to snare its prey, he hisses a series of arousing expletives into my ear, bites me harder, whilst ordering me to silence my pretty, little mouth. I try to stifle a weak whimper, but alas said sound has plans of its own and it rapidly exits from my mouth. He murmurs something inaudible under his breath, quickly releases me from his hold and without any warning, once again, he sinks his teeth into me but this time, he leaves that particular secret love-note imprinted deep within the flesh that coats my left buttock.

I wail out with an agonizing scream at that mark of his!

"Mine?" he moans, his voice tinged with a plea.

"Yours," I sigh.

Retracting from me, I angle my head over my shoulder and I take in a deep breath for what I see is his hand sweeping through the heavily-musky scented air. As his palm impacts with my skin, he drapes his body over me and thrusts his cock deep into my aching core. I turn, his warm hands settle upon the roundness of my shoulders, and he slowly eases them down until my face is flush with the pillow. I turn my head to left and rest my cheek upon the soft fabric. Blanketing his body with mine, he nips my earlobe and sensually breathes, "You're perfect, Helena. Just so, so desirably perfect."

While my hands claw for a hold on the silk sheeting, he slides effortlessly in and out of me, winding my ponytail around his fist, he angles my head backwards and I in response to his delectable dominance, let out an airless breath. Starting to set the rhythm, he grips me firm around my waist and sinks his body so deep into me that I am sure I can feel his cock pulsating through my belly

Another silent wail envelopes me.

As each powerful pistoning of his manhood stretches me, fills me beyond a belief, I find myself now only left with the ability to feel every inch of him claiming, consuming the person that is his.

Me.

While Darius hums away in the shower, my curiosity takes hold of me and I wonder what is behind the red velvet curtains at the far end of the suite. As I pull them apart and step inside, confusion reigns over me. I see that one half of this vast closet is filled with a selection of business suits, an array of dress shirts while the opposite half houses more casual attire. I look lower to the shoe rails and I see different shades and styles oxfords after oxfords… On the dress-down side there are numerous converse trainers and other relaxed footwear. My mind now in a total whirl as to whose room we have invaded and more so, to whose bed we have just left infused with the musky scent of our recent passion fuelled, sex session, I walk back to the bed and seat myself. My inquisitive nature now fully fledged, I pull open the bedside drawer. My stomach cramps when I see two boxes of condoms. One reads – Ultrathin for maximum sensation, and the other – Extra finely ribbed for her pleasure.

Passing them by, I also come across a variety of sexual lubricants that are contained within conical shaped glass bottles. Strewn around the drawer is a cache of sex toys, one being a string of glass anal beads. On catching sight of a scrunched up piece of paper that appears to have been stuffed into the rear right corner, the images of the usage of said sex toy quickly vanishes from my mind. I now gingerly place my hand inside, fleeting over the items, and I pinch the paper between my thumb and forefinger. Extracting it, I place it upon my trembling knees, smooth it open, and when I read the scribbles written, I have to swallow extremely hard.

Thank you for sex previous, Mr Carter.
And yes, sir, you have left your mark upon me.
The only man, who will ever be allowed to touch me, will
always be you.
Alice
X

As my head spins, my sub conscious hits me with a barrage of questions;

Hasn't it dawned on you that this room you're in is his fuck pad?

Why do you think he had his own personal parking space in the car park?

Didn't you notice the name on the plaque that was inscribed? Mr Darius Carter?

It wasn't by chance there was a free convenient park close to the elevator! He's chosen that space for a fast entry and a quick exit!

Why do think he never had to book you both in at reception?

Why do you think the closets are full of his attire?

Why do you think the contents of the drawer are close to hand?

This is the place he brings women to fuck!

Get out! Get out! Helena! You must leave for there's a traitor about!

(Well, the double-crosser's still in the shower, but I'd make haste if I was you!)

You're worth better than this.

...Connor?

After rapidly dressing, I find my handbag, sling it over my shoulder and without further ado, I slam the door firmly shut behind me. Making it to the car park, I run through it as fast as I can and with my mind now in a total whirl, I swear my feet barely touched the ground at all. On exiting the park, as I turned the corner, I see a black taxi cab approaching, so I outstretch my arm and hail for it to halt. In a matter of moments it does. I still and watch the window open. As the driver asks, "Where would you like to go Miss?"

Home – *I tell him, I want to go home.*

Settling myself into the back seat, as the car motors off, I gratefully slump back into the seat, close my eyelids. As the tears sting the back of my eyes, I try to push the whole damn mess that had just occurred to the back of my mind. Mentally forcing the ghastly thoughts to go away, my cell buzzes. I yank it out of my jean pocket, and glance at it to see Darius name imprinted across the screen. This is the conversation that transpired:

I understand why you left so abruptly, but where are you? I need, I wish to explain about the items that you stumbled across.

I'm going as far away from you as I possibly can.

Why so far away? I'm confused.

Confused? I doubt it! I imagine you're lying on your bed surrounded by an abundance of fuck toys, and that... that awful note from that woman called Alice! Or maybe you've already called her up and she is on her way over to soothe your fevered brow!

No I am not! I am dressed, feeling perplexed and standing right next to my car actually! And for your information, Helena, I wouldn't do such a thing as to call her. She IS PAST HISTORY.

Past? Past enough to still be hiding in a draw waiting to be resurrected by you?

It's an old note – it means nothing – you mean everything to me – You are my world now, Helena.

Funnily enough, I don't believe you. What do you actually want from me? What do you want me to do? Submit and scamper back to you?

Basically, yes, I do. Please come back. I owe you an explanation about the things you fell across. Please, Helena, come to me and we can talk face-to-face?

Fuck off!

Excuse me?

Double fuck off!

Mouth, Helena!

Triple fuck off!

Extremely angry at your foul words but considering the circumstances as to why you are spouting at me in that unladylike fashion, I am doing my best to ignore obnoxious responses! Now, calm down and tell me exactly where you are.

Not far enough away from you yet, you two-timing, cheating rat!

I will find you. You're not leaving me without giving me a chance to explain.

You will find me considering you know where I live and work but know this, Darius – In my heart I have already left you.

HELENA!

GO AWAY!

HELENA? PLEASE TALK TO ME. I'M BEGGING YOU, PLEASE?

PLEAD ALL YOU LIKE...YOU MEAN NOTHING TO ME. WE ARE OVER!

WHAT? NEVER!

WHAT PART OF WE.ARE.OVER. DON'T YOU UNDERSTAND?

Please, Helena, at least before you leave me give me a chance to explain?

Too late!

What do you mean by too late?

I've already told you – I've left you. Goodbye, Darius.

One minute later:

Helena?

One minute and thirty seconds later:

Helena are you there?

Two minutes later:

Helena?

Two minutes and thirty seconds later:

Helena, please talk to me. I'm so sorry.

After I read his final plea, I felt completely void and with nothing left to offer him, I felt like I had no option but to turn my phone off.

Sagging back into the seat, I put my phone on mute and for a weak moment, I ponder whether I wish to go home or not. I think about deciding upon the latter. Somehow I don't want to be alone right at this particular moment in time. I guess I could call Connor up for company – *maybe if I'm still feeling lonely, later I might.* As the taxi cab motors on, I close my eyes and drift off. I think of nothing until I hear the driver say that we have arrived at my home. I promptly settle my fare and head towards the safety of my apartment. As the night drifted into early morning, I showered, dressed, breakfasted and prepared myself for work. I didn't eat much, mainly just toyed around with a bowl of cereal. I can tell you that there were times during the night when I considered calling up Darius and giving him a chance to explain but I felt right now, at that particular moment in time, I wouldn't be ready to listen to what he had to say. I just need more than time; I need to get back to reality. So, on this bleakest of mornings, I close my front door, and make headway to the underground, board the tube and settle into the twenty-minute journey to work.

CHAPTER TWENTY-SEVEN

The Florists

With her face now reddening with anger, Angelica hands me a Kleenex and curses, "He did what to you?

"He... he... two-timed me," I sniff.

She mutters a string of obscenities under her breath and then asks, "And what did you find exactly lurking in the bedside drawer?"

I loudly blow my nose into the paper tissue; choke back a sob and say, "Two packs of condoms, some... some, sex toys and a note from, from..."

Her voice softer, she gently soothes, "From whom, Helena? Who was the note from? You can tell me."

"It... It... was from, some woman called, Alice," I heave.

"Would you like to tell me what it said?"

I recite, word for word the following written below to Angelica and while she listens in silence, my tears start to freely flow.

Thank you for sex previous, Mr Carter.
And yes, sir, you have left your mark upon me.
The only man, who will ever be allowed to touch me, will
always be you.
Alice
X

With my body now racking with sobs, Angelica places her hands upon my shoulder, holds me firm and then hits me hard with her response.

"So it would seem that the conniving bastard lured you into his fuck pad, then soft soaped you with an abundance of heartfelt words and then… then," she growls, "after… after he had made love to you, with you, while he was showering his false love for you down the plughole, bubbles and all, that was the moment when you discovered all of this horrifying information?"

I hold back another impending sob and whimper a meek – yes.

"The cheating rat!" she wails. "He had better not come near you ever again. I'm going to tell Xavier what he's done."

"Please don't," I sob. "Don't bring Xavier into this mess."

"Okay," she agrees but then launches, "If I find out that he's attempted to contact you, I'll hunt him down and I will give him more than a piece of my mind… I'll thwack the cocky arsehole!"

"Please don't, Angelica." I plead. "I just want to forget that I ever… ever…"

"Ever let yourself be duped by him?"

"Yes." I murmur. "Tricked into believing he loved me and only me."

"Well it's too late for that, isn't it, to forget or even to forgive?"

"Please stop this conversation now." I beg. "It was a mistake… I won't forgive him, that I can assure you of. And… and," I cry, "It's all turned into one giant, horrible mess that I'd rather, if you don't mind, forget."

She gives me a sympathetic look, tells me that she's sorry for her outburst but she's just so cross that I'm hurting, that I have been hurt. I tell her that it's all right and that I wouldn't have expected anything less from my best friend. She then suggests that maybe I should forego work today and head back home. I shake my head as to signal a no and with my tears now over, I pull myself together and say, "What am I going to do at home, Angelica? Just sit there, brooding, crying a little more over Mr mad-hatter dickhead and his Alice-in-wonderland tart?"

She grins at my description of Darius and Alice – *Darius and Alice* – I feel nauseas at the thought of him with another – and says, "No, I guess that's probably not the best option in aiding a broken heart. Maybe keeping busy is better. Distraction can ease this sorrow a little I guess?"

Picking up the clipboard from the table, I swing my legs around and hop off the stool, I tell her that nothing will ease my sorrow at present and I add that as far as I'm concerned Mr Carter – the two-timing cheating rat – never existed.

I hear her mumble, "Okay, Helena," If this is how you want to deal with this then you do exactly that.

I sigh, and say that I will head off out back and start the stock check. I can't face customers today. She nods in understanding and in agreement and so, as I step out back, the shop phone rings and thus this most fateful of days begins. The tinkling of the bell above the shop door signals to me that someone has entered, so I shout, "Angelica, I believe we have a customer."

"I'm on the phone" she hollers back. "Will you help them?"

I inwardly groan. I have no choice but to oblige, so I head out into the shop front, look up from my itinerary and straight into the piercing, steely-blue eyes of one extremely tired looking Darius. He looks like he hasn't slept all night and judging by the shadowy growth of dark hair that's gracing his jawline, I'm guessing he's probably not bothered to either bathe. Surveying his crumpled jeans and t-shirt, I frown and nervously stammer, "What, what are you doing here? Why are you here?"

He furrows his brow, rubs his forehead and without a moment's hesitation, he replies, "I've come to take you back with me."

Now reeling on the spot at the shocking audacity of this man, my clipboard falls from my grasp and hits the floor. Bending down to pick it up, I woefully reply, "After yesterday, I don't ever want to be in close proximity to you."

With concern in his voice, he crouches on the spot and asks me to look at him. For some reason I do exactly as he wishes.

"Your eyes look a little bloodshot, Helena. Have you been crying?"

"No, it's... it's... the pollen," I lie. "The... the pollen in the air making my eyes appear dewy."

Now looking back to the floor, I scoop up my clipboard and we both rise to our feet. I take a brief glance at him. His shoulders are sagging and his look is forlorn. He lunges at me, grasps my arm and I shudder at the electrifying touch of his hand upon my bare flesh. Pulling away as quickly as I can from him, I watch him run his shaking hand through his hair. Tousling his curls, he then flashes me an award winning smile while soulfully whispering, "Never... Are you one hundred percent sure of that? You never want to see me, hold me or touch me ever again?"

I pause – I shouldn't have hesitated, but nevertheless I did giving time for these thoughts to infiltrate my mind. *Of course I do. I want nothing more than to fall into your waiting arms again but the shock, the emotional trauma of what I discovered yesterday evening in your fuck pad has left me not only cautious of you but now I have to closely guard my heart and stop you from shattering any it further.*

Mentally forcing these thoughts to abate and thankfully they did, I regain my composure and lock eyes with him. Hoping that he won't hear the quiver in the back of my throat, I affirm to him that I never, ever want to see or hear from him ever again. He arches an eyebrow and suggests that maybe I am being a little hasty in my decision and would I at least go for a coffee with him and give him a chance to explain. I quite simply decline. I don't want to be with him – well I do – but I can't be close to him for another touch of his person upon mine, I know I will weaken and fall into his arms. He really surprises me when turns on his heel and heads towards the door. On reaching the exit, he spins around and at that point I am informed by him that as I appear to be ninety-nine percent sure of never wanting to see him again he will never darken my door again but one thing he will most definitely do is he never forget me.

I will never forget you either, Darius… Ever.

Rushing to the window seat, I settle myself down curl up upon the cushions. He's now ambling towards his car with his hands stuffed into his jean pockets. His head is bowed. While he walks with the stance of a man who seems to be lost in a state of limbo, I want to do nothing more than to run out into the street and catch up with him and tell him that I will listen to his confession/admittance. So, while I debate whether I should or not do the latter, I hear Angelica dropping the catch on the front door. I look over and see her turning the sign over that informs customers that we are open to shut. She comes over to me, seats herself down, and takes my hand in hers.

"I saw and heard what just happened, Helena."

"You did? And, what are your thoughts?"

"The man is obviously smitten with you."

"You really think so?"

"Truly I do."

"Why, do you think this?"

"Because of the last sentence he said to you."

The moment before I burst into a fit of uncontrollable tears, and cried solidly for an hour into Angelica's arms, I whispered to Darius through the glass window that I will never forget him either. And the last glimpse I caught of him was him checking his blind spot before motoring off at an incredibly fast speed.

CHAPTER TWENTY-EIGHT

De La Margherita Restaurant

Le Saxonophist

Six Months Later

The open shirted, dark haired man standing on the tiny sawdust encrusted podium at the back of this bijou eatery Connor and I are in, loudly claps his hands together. Now having rapidly gained the eaters' attention, he then taps his highly polished saxophone and slowly, as the chitter chatter of the diners' ceases into a low murmur, he then causes the majority of us to leap in our seats when he booms, "I need a couple of star-crossed lovers to dance to my music. Who will do me the honour? Who would be willing enough to compliment my song with a brave display of expressive body language?"

As a rumble of murmurs turn into a hushed silence, no one takes up his offer, and as he asks again, he points over in the direction of Connor and me. Gentlemanly bowing to us, he then suggests, "What about the beautiful bella sitting over in the corner with her handsome blonde Adonis?"

While chatter reverberates through the garlicky infused air, I feel as if the entire persons in the room are staring at us. Focusing upon the saxophonist, as he sweeps his hand through the air, with such professionalism he coerces the audience and asks, "Do you all agree that the fiery red-headed bella and the freckled Adonis should dance for us?"

Laughter is soon followed by a roar of yes which in turn is succeeded by the chink of wine goblets meeting and the sound of cutlery scraping against crockery.

"Oh, damn it, Connor," I whisper. "This is so embarrassing. We're not even a couple."

He pulls an extremely sad face, murmurs that he wished we were and replies, "These dear people don't know that, do they? Come on, let's dance. Let's show everyone some of our hot, sexy moves!"

Taking a large sip of San Pellegrino water, I swallow and sigh, "No, I guess they don't know that we are not together, so…"

"So? Wanna show the punters what you're made of? Wanna get up and shake that tight booty of yours at them?"

I giggle at his choice of words and he rises from his seat, grins and offers me his hand.

"Come on, fiery red-headed Bella! Your freckled Adonis needs you!"

"No," I whisper. "I can't… I won't. It's a stupid idea!"

"Oh, don't be such a killjoy, Ellie; it's just a bit of harmless fun! And come on, be honest, when did you last have any fun? All you've done for the last six months since *he* fucked you off is work, work, work and you know the saying, all work and no play makes Bella a dull beauty!"

True. Since I left Darius, I am becoming a withered rose.

I frown, and only uncrease my brow when he winks at me and adds, "No strings attached, my-apple-queen. I promise I won't even attempt to kiss you."

Shame…

I smile at his words and by the way a pleading look has spread across his face, I give in to his ask and to be truthful, quite frankly, I've become rather tired of worrying and fretting over Darius, so I guess this is the right moment to start living again. I accept his hand, and he helps me to my feet. Drawing me into him, he takes my left hand in his while placing the palm of his right hand flush to the curve at the lower of my spine, I settle my hand upon his right shoulder. As the saxophonist starts to play and the notes of the sexy tones fill the Chianti infiltrated air; I feel an all too familiar charge shift between Connor and me.

"Hey, baby?" he purrs. "Did you feel something strange surround us?"

While we sway and the onlookers, in between their mouthfuls of food and over-generous sips of wine, briefly glance at us, I want to tell Connor that I did indeed feel what he felt but something's preventing me from disclosing, so I just inch a little closer into him and keep my lips sealed – *for now.* The music rises and falls, and within the secret romance of the instruments' notes, I feel like I am going burst out into tears. Connor senses my wavering and holds me firm, and I lose myself even further when he whispers over and over into my ear that he… he… still loves me. I am now so lost within translation, so vulnerable in affairs of the heart, that when a familiar voice splits between us and asks, "May I break this dance?"

… I feel as if all of the air has been just be vacuumed out of my lungs.

My knees buckle and Connor, sensing that I am now unnerved by the whole scenario, grips me firm around the waist and steadies me. We are then again politely questioned if he may stop us dancing together and as he does the gentle tones of his question settle upon my soul and it slowly dawns upon me who he may be. I release from Connor's hold, and turn my head. Rolling my eyes to the right, as I see the owner of said voice standing tall before me, I don't know whether to flee or stay put. The reason for my confusion is there he is…

Darius.

On seeing him for the first time in six months, I feel as if I have been punched hard in the gut and the pain of that sharp, short blow has been multiplied and intensified in its agony.

His lips are set into a firm, thin line and his eyes, well I've never seen them appear so lacklustre. His jawline is camouflaged by a well-groomed beard and that silky dark mass of manly facial hair only serves to strip back another layer of my protective defence. Oh how I want to feel him nuzzling into the crook of my neck. Pushing the thoughts of him to the rear of my mind, I sidle up to Connor and he slips his hand in mine. Squeezing my shaking palm tight, he whispers to me that everything is going to be fine and then with such authority in his voice, he protectively says, "No, you can't cut in and have this dance, Carter. Ellie wants nothing to do with you ever again."

Darius doesn't utter a word in response. He just fleets his stare from Connor to me and then back again. Repeating his actions twice more, he then finally stills and transfixes upon Connor. While he glares at him hard, I look away from Darius because, I can't bear to look at the man I loved any longer, for if I do, I know I will take a step forward, fling myself into his arms and melt into his white tee shirted, taut chest. Looking at the floor, I focus upon his converse trainers, and while I try to mentally unravel the knots on his laces, I hear Connor ask him to do the right thing by me and please would he leave. Moments pass so agonisingly slowly. Darius still remains silent. And I remain mute. The air is now charged with strangulated electricity and I am seriously considering exiting the building- alone. As I confirm to myself that that is exactly what I should do, said converse trainers shuffle, turn and vanish from my vision. I raise my lashes to see Darius, his back towards me, his hands stuffed into his jean pockets ambling out of the door.

"He's gone," I soulfully mutter. "He's really gone?"

"I'm sorry, Ellie, yes, he's gone."

"I... I..." I sniff. "I wanted to... to..."

"You wanted to do what, Ellie?"

"Nothing. Just nothing Connor, forget it. I want to go home."

"Share a cab?"

"Not tonight. I just want to be alone."

"You will call me if you need anything."

"I promise I will."

After hugging Connor good night, and promising that I will have lunch with him tomorrow, as the chilliness of the mid-evening sets in, I wrap my knitted cardigan around me. Fumbling into the left hand pocket I locate my set of keys. Extracting them, I select the key to my precious battered old mini and insert said key into the lock. As I turn it I freeze, for out of the thin air a voice pleaded,

"Please just give me one chance to explain about everything, Helena. Just one chance and I promise after I've said what I have to say that I will leave you in peace."

I spun on my heel to see Darius standing before me. Under the illumination of the streetlights he looked positively stunning. His dark hair was its usual crop of an unruly mess – maybe a tad longer that normal and the smooth facial hair that creates his beard, shimmered under the artificial lighting that was allowing me to see him clearer.

With my heart thumping in my chest, I took a deep breath and declared, "If you talk to me, Darius, I might just crumble before you." He batted his lashes at me and I continued. "You might see me come undone unravel before your very eyes. Is that what you want to see? Me belittled before you once again?"

Stuffing his hands into his jean pockets, he shook his head from side to side, sighed no and replied, "I want to see none of those things. I... I…wish… I… wish that we… we…"

With curiosity in my voice, I asked, "What do you wish for then? What exactly do you want from me?"

He took a few steps towards me and I retreated back against my car, all the while anticipating feeling the hedonistic sensation of his lips upon mine. On reaching me he outstretched his arms and pressed his palms flush either side of my head. Resting his hands upon the roof of the car, he leant into me, pressed his forehead to mine and in the clearest of voices declared, "I want you back."

Before I could respond, his warm lips were upon mine, and I didn't resist against him. Once again I became lost within the sweet infusions of his mouth. While this most passionate and loving of kisses began rekindling the love we had/still have for each other, I tried with all my might to resist falling for him again – truth be told, I know that I never stopped loving him – he then stunned me when broke away, gazed deep into my eyes, and with such sincerity in his voice, finally told me what I'd been aching to hear over the lonely months without him. "I love you."

My mind now in a total whirl, needing to hear him say those three little words to me again, I told him that I didn't quite hear what he said. Furrowing his brow, seeming a little confused to me, he dipped his lashes and repeated,

"I love you."

"Do you love me just now because you can't have me or have you always loved me?"

Flicking his eyelids open, he focused intently at me and spoke. "I have loved you before I was even created."

"How much do you love me?"

"My love for you is immeasurable."

"If you loved me back then, like you do now why, oh why, oh why did you take me to your... your... that place?"

"It wasn't planned," he sighed. "Remember we were in a heated argument and it was pure coincidence that we passed the car park and I needed to cool down or we may have had an accident.

"Okay, fair enough, I understand that but why did you take me into that apartment and bed me in a bed that you have seduced other women in?"

"Helena, you had me crazed. All I could think after you were at my feet on the cold stone floor answering my stupid jealous questions while crying and all I could think about was taking you to bed and making you mine."

"Couldn't you have thought about just taking me back to your condo?"

"With hindsight, yes, that's what I should've done. I'm sorry."

"And her? What about Alice?"

That was the moment when he recoiled from me and his face turned an ashen shade.

"I won't talk about her here out in the open but if you would come back home with me, I'll explain everything to you."

"Everything? You'll answer truthfully any questions I have to ask."

He gave a curt nod and then he completely flummoxed me when he offered me his hand and said one word and that word was – come.

I went.

CHAPTER TWENTY-NINE

Perched on the kitchen stool, as I watch Darius slide out a bottle of wine from the fridge rack, I can't help but stare at his t-shirt cladded back. My vision travels over the top of his broad muscular shoulders, down past the centre of his back, and I now find myself shamelessly imagining what it would once again be like to be pinned beneath him while he claims both my body and soul. I am broken from my inappropriate thoughts when he turns around to face me, holds up a chilled bottle and asks, "Would you like a glass of this rather delicious fresh, fruity rosé wine before we start?"

Mesmerised by him with that gorgeous, silken beard of his, I can't utter a word, so I nod as to signal yes because not only does that particular bottle that he is holding contain my most favourite of wines, but right now I could most certainly do with a glass or two of it to spear me with the courage that I need to listen to what he has to say. Seating himself opposite me, he pours us both a generous measure of the liquid and we simultaneously take the first of tastes. Mirroring each other we place our glasses down onto the marble work surface and I stare at the label on the bottle.

Domaine Ott Romassan Rose Bandol.

Looking over at him, I smile, "That's my favourite French wine, Darius."

Arching an eyebrow, he smiles back, "I know."

"How do you know?" I exclaim. "I've most certainly never told you?"

"There are lots of bits and pieces I know about you, Helena. In fact, I've made it my mission in life to know every single little detail about you."

Next, for some strange reason I blurt out, "I've always wanted to visit France."

He picks up his glass, inhales the bouquet that houses a combination of peach, lemon, cinnamon and vanilla aromas, and without taking his vision off me, he amuses, "You've never been to France?"

"No... I've never been." I sigh, take a sip and as the liquid touches my lips and the coolness tingles on my tongue, I relish in the flavour of its fresh summer fruitiness.

"Well I'll have to rectify that by taking you there one day and making love to you in the fragrant lavender fields of Provence."

Circling the rim of my glass, I stare into the goblet and mutter a "That would've been nice."

"Would've? Why are you're talking past tense to me. You don't see a future for us ahead even though I told you less than an hour ago that I loved you?"

"I... I... Don't know, Darius. This, the past... It's all so very puzzling for me right now."

He takes both out glasses, arranges them to one side and leans over the counter. Taking both my hands in his, he upturns them and strokes his fingers along my palms. "I know it's confusing for you right now to trust me let alone even be with me but please, Helena, I implore you to come and sit with me on the sofa and let me explain about the fateful day when you left me and I broke apart."

He was hurting too?

Seated opposite each other, Darius strokes the soft, dark hair that graces his chin and asks, "Are you sitting comfortably, Helena?"

Sitting cross-legged I tell him that I am and please could he now begin his explanation. Without a hint of expression upon his face, he tells me that when he divulges the truth, he would prefer it if I did not interrupt him during his speech, and he will answer any questions that I have when he has finished explaining everything that there is to know. *Okay* – He parts his lips, opens his mouth and I listen intently as the truth tumbles forth.

"Approximately two years before you fell into my world, I purchased what you crudely have referred to, as my fuck pad."

"Well it is what it is!" I quip. "It's a horrible, ghastly…"

He frowns and I snap my mouth shut. Taking another taste of his wine, he swallows, draws in a breath and continues.

"I have never been the type of man who finds it easy to scour the field for female company, so in order to satisfy my sexual needs, I… I… I used…"

I take a large gulp of wine and with my curiosity now peaked, I have to refrain from asking – you used what? Running his fingers through his curls, he resumes,

"…The services of an elite escort agency. An agency so discreet that they are only known by word of mouth. I would have a lady sent to up to me as and when I required. Sometimes I would finance for her to stay one for one night, sometimes two but most definitely never three.

Why never three?

Twenty-four hours in the company of a female was always enough to satisfy my needs. Thirty-six hours however, would only serve to breed a certain type of intimacy that would entail ruses of a romantic nature and back then, I wasn't in it for love – Just sex.

Just vanilla sex or kinkier?

"I know what you're thinking, Helena, and the answer is plain old fashioned Vanilla."

I shrug my shoulders and he shakes his head from side to side.

"So," he pauses and then asks, "Are you ready to hear the next part of my story?"

Yes.

One day, six months or so into my adventures with the escort agency, I asked for them to pair me with a lady who was interested in one of my hobbies – photography. They did. Her name was…" he sighs, "was… Alice. Over time, Alice and I became what you would call, close. I broke my golden rule and became personally involved with her. She had a certain magnetic charm about her and I was powerless to resist its force. As we became fond of one another events took an uncanny twist and within the innocence of her surprise submission, I discovered that I was displaying thoughts that pertained to dominant behaviour. I had never before entertained the fact that there was a mere soupçon of dominancy within me, but she discovered it within me and ignited the blue touch paper and," He wafts his hands in the air and I almost fall of my stool when he declares, "Voila! I, the gentle dominant was born."

I take a breath and quiz, "So…So… It's her fault that you are the way that you are?"

"And what do you mean by that, Helena?"

"I… I… mean that she made you… turned you into a dominant?"

"No." And with a strict seriousness in his voice, he without hesitation tells me this. "I believe that I have always had hidden dominant tendencies. It was fate that she had to be the woman to unleash, unravel – whatever you wish to call it – extract me from within my dark prison."

"Do you like being a dominant?"

"What do you think, Helena?"

"I... I... think that you do. I think that it is a fundamental part of your physical and mental makeup."

"Explain."

"Well this is how I see you. You are a man who is extremely disciplined in all manner of things."

"Yes I am. Now may I continue?"

I nod. He resumes.

"I would see, Ali... *her*... on Friday evening through to the Sunday ending our time together at six p.m. If I needed a sexual release during the week, I would of course take to pleasuring myself. As I became more and more sexually replete with her weekend visits, the need for satisfaction during the week began to peter out. One Wednesday, after days and days of rehearsing one short scene, a scene that eluded me, it was finally in the can. I was so hyped, so driven that I needed a release, and of course being the middle of the week, she was out of bounds, or so I thought so. I drove to my pad, indulged in a relaxing bath and then finally settled down in bed. I then selected a pornographic movie, and I viewed it will the full intent of ... Well I think you can guess what I mean, Helena."

I can!

"After satisfying myself, I took a cold shower – no need to explain why. While I was under the jets of water, unbeknown to me, Alice had let herself in the room. What happened that night within the confines of my room, you do not need to know, but all I can say is that the note you saw from her to me was written upon that day. Two years before I met you at the premiere."

A hushed silence fills the room and as I process what he has just explained to me, I look away from him and shakily ask, "Where… where is she now?"

He takes another taste of his wine, raises his shoulders briefly and responds, "I do not know where she is and neither do I wish too."

"Oh I see. Can you tell me why you broke up with her?"

"Do you really need to know why we parted?"

"Yes, I do."

"We parted." He closes his eyes momentarily and as he opens them he breathes, "Because I couldn't give her what she wanted."

"What couldn't you give her?"

He looks at me and I shiver as he answers, "The whole package."

"I don't understand what you mean by that Darius?"

"Then let me spell it out for you. I didn't want to get married back then and I certainly didn't wish to father children."

"And now what do you wish for?"

Rising from his seat, he approaches me, and rests his hands firmly upon my shoulders. And whispers,

"I wish for you to be mine."

"In what way do you want me to be yours? Do you want me to be your girlfriend, or/and your submissive?" I pause, he stills and then as the word – *wife?* tumbles from my lips, his eyes mist over. He's now transfixed upon me, whispering that he wants me to be first and foremost my last word to him. I'm now weakening inside at the vision of this tall, dark, handsome man standing before me who wishes for me to be Mrs Carter and while the fresh scent of his persona once again penetrates and infuses my senses, I part my lips in anticipation for one of his heart melting kisses. He knowingly smiles. Maintaining eye contact with me, he slowly trails his hands down my arms and the combination of his magnetic aura coupled with the delicacy of his touch both cause me to feel light headed.

"I... I..." I mutter, "I... I... Did... did... did... you just ask me... me... to... to.... mar... marry..."

I can't set final words that I wish to express to him free from my soul and he senses this by affirming to me an understanding nod.

"Shhh, my darling Helena," falls from his bowed lips.

I immediately quiet.

"There is no need for any words to be exchanged right now," he softly whispers, and then adds, "None at all."

I couldn't agree more with him, for if I was able offer my thoughts to him; they would be projected as nothing more than a jumbled mess of undecipherable sentences. On reaching my trembling hands, he makes no hesitation in entwining his fingers with mine. As our skins meets, I find myself being drawn into his taut chest. Burying my head into him, he tenderly strokes my hair, and breathes, "Now that I've found you, Helena," his voice weakens and he murmurs, "I'm never going to let you stray from me again... Even," he hushes, "Even if it means putting a ring on your finger."

He's asking me to marry him?

I look up at him and I'm totally confused at this whole scenario, so for the moment I choose to say nothing about his impromptu proposal. On spotting a lone tear trickling down his cheek, from my heart, I respond,

"Now that you've located me, Darius, I don't... don't want to be apart from you ever... ever again."

"Am I forgiven then?"

"Yes," I affirm. "I wholeheartedly pardon you for your past behaviour."

His torso heaves heavily with a sigh that is filled with a burst of relief and I respond by standing on my tippy-toes, breaking my hands free from his, and flinging them around his neck. While I hold onto to him, never wishing to ever let go, he seals this moment in time by whispering to me a secret – *One that I have yet to unravel.*

CHAPTER THIRTY

Wonderland

Settling his naked, taut body over me, Darius' warm lips skim lightly over my throat – I'm free-falling. And while his mouth travels down the centre of my cleavage, and the heat of his breath warms my flesh, I arch my back and part my legs in anticipation for his body entering mine. My voice is light and wispy, and I breathe, "That feels so good, baby. I've missed your gentle touch so much."

He looks up at me, weakens me a spine tingling slow bat of his lashes and then bows his head. His lips are now clamped around my erecting nipple and he, with such intensity draws upon it, coaxing it into a hardness that I have never experienced before. As a series of sensitive tingles radiate through my hips and collate at my now dampening centre, I moan out his name with such intensity. Continuing the onslaught upon my breast, he asks,

"You want me to stop, Helena, or do you want to experience some more of my sensual teasing?"

Angling my hips up towards him, I whimper out, more.

He fleets a glance at me and with his forearm now pressing into the silk covered mattress; he suckles away upon my flesh, slides his hand between my thighs and I burn inside when he says, "You're mine, Helena. Don't ever forget that."

With my inner core aching for his touch, "Yes," I hiss between my clenched teeth. "I'm yours, Darius. I won't forget."

He's now released me from his hold, shuffled up and we are face to face. Gripping a fistful of my hair in his hand, he caresses my tresses, dips his head and while his beard tickles my face, he seals his mouth over mine. His tongue is hot and delectably moist and as it darts around mine, a series of needy, wanting sounds rise from both our souls. Clasping my buttocks, his hips circling, with one powerful propulsion of his midriff, he is fully inside me and I, well I have instantly become lost within him. His voice is soft and syrupy, he drawls his words long and slow, and he has my undivided attention when he warns, "Be prepared, Helena, for this is not only going to be a long, slow sexual onslaught of skin upon skin, it is also going to be the deepest, the hardest you have ever felt me inside you."

He was correct in his assumption, for he is grinding into me so forcefully that my nails are trailing down the sides of his back and I am 'hanging' on for dear life.

Rocking me hard, in between each on one of his upward thrusts, he pants, "Where are you, my precious? Tell me where you are."

With my orgasm threatening, I shudder and wail, "I am with you."

"Good. Now dig deeper into me," he demands. "When we come in unison, I want to feel you leaving your mark on me."

On the final thrust of his cock inside me, as he cried out my name in a way that I have never heard before, I did indeed leave my imprint upon his beautiful body. As we shuddered, shook and slid against each other there was no need for any more words because intimacy and the power of touch had prevailed.

THIS IS NO WONDERLAND

On waking, much to my disappointment, I find that I am alone in bed. While I adjust to the new day, I must admit, I am feel slightly heady and a little delicate between my legs. *Thank you Darius!* On catching a whiff of the aroma of coffee brewing, I relax back into the cushions that surround me. With the aromatic scent of the dark beans alerting me to the fact that I have located Darius, I smile at the thought of him preparing breakfast for two. While I reminisce at the sensual and erotic thoughts of our recent love-making, I smile with a divine pure happiness. I am now so engrossed in reliving the moment when we both declared our love for each other, that I can just about make out the ascending sound of a cell buzzing within the room. As it loudens and raps ferociously against the surface of his bedside table, demanding to be noticed, I groan out and mentally insert my private thoughts into an imaginary box. Tying said box up with a make-believe red ribbon, I secure both the ends into a bow and lay said box down to rest, *well for now.* Turning onto my side, I grasp his pillow and scrunch it up to my nose. Inhaling the scent of his manliness that has been left impregnated deep within the cotton fibres, I hold onto the breath for as long as I can; arousing at his fragrance, as moments pass by, I am soon left with no choice but to let that most precious of breaths escape. *His phone continues interrupting!* As I do, it whooshes out from my lungs, and Darius enters my mind. On the thought of him, I press my thighs together. *Ow!* Very tender indeed! Outstretching my arm, I locate the irritating, intrusive phone, slide it off the table-top and flop onto my back. With his pillow now resting upon my bare chest and his phone now firmly in my grasp, I linger it above my face. Blinking a couple of times, as the screen comes into focus and the caller's title flashes back at me, my all-to-brief perfect moment implodes and I am propelled into a state of a blind-panicking trauma. Feeling like I am alone, in a dingy that has been bobbing about on the roughest of seas for days, my stomach begins to violently churn and my hands tremor. The reason for display of fear and the uncomfortable sensation of nausea is that the five letters on the screen staring back me, taunting me with its now silence has a name and that name *is*:

Alice.

This is no wonderland that I have been left suspended in. It is in fact pure torture.

EPILOGUE

Taking a sip of my coffee, I place the mug down onto the table top and pick up this morning's newspaper. When I see the headline strewn across the top of the front page, I feel sick to the inner core for it is informing me that Darius, the man I am still in love with, while filming on location in Italy, has been involved in a motorbike accident. As I continue reading, the printed words bring to my attention that he is in ITC and that his condition is life-threatening. Reciting his phone number off by heart, I glance at the time on my own cell, 7.36 a.m. I dial…

ITALY

Three months later
8.36 a.m.
DARIUS

I force my eyelids to open and as they do, I can just about make out some vague shapes surrounding me. This experience is all very alien to me and I'm feeling extremely frightened, *Where are you, Helena? I need you by my side.*
"Stats?" I hear a male's, muffled voice from faraway ask.
"There are none. Dr Franco." A female's voice responds.

Flatline.

THE LIGHT WITHIN THE DARKNESS

Darius

Time of my death – 8.36a.m

"Helena?"
"Yes, Darius?"
"I want to tell you that I will love you for eternity and if there is anything beyond that, then I will love you in that most magical and mystical of places too."
"I love you too, baby. Stay strong. I'm coming for you."
"I will try, but please hurry without you by my side I don't think I can breathe let alone return."
"I'm flying now."
"I'm running towards you now…"

From the distance I hear a loud blip followed by another and then another. With a rhythm maintaining, I hear the briefest of conversations wisp over me…

"Dr Franco?"
"Yes, Sister Mary?"
"We have a faint pulse."

Time of my rebirth – 8.37 a.m.

'QUANTUM ENTANGLEMENT'

DARIUS AND HELENA'S STORY CONTINUES IN THE
ROMANTICALLY SENSUAL AND POWERFULLY EROTIC
SECOND NOVEL IN THE GENTLE DOMINANT SERIES

CHRISTMAS EVE 2016
11.47p.m.
To lovers everywhere around the world – Romantic souls
who are lost and waiting to found

JL Thomas.

"The truth is that airports have seen more sincere kisses than
the wedding halls, and the walls of hospitals have heard
more prayers than the walls of a church."

As the humming sound of aircraft passing by above us sings through the winter's air, the chill of the joyful season's offering stings our faces. I draw in an icy breath of oxygen, and as I feel the man, who against all odds has cheated death snaking his leather gloved hands under my cloak, I shudder with a mixture of a great sense of relief and anticipation. Darius then takes the lead by curling his arms around my tiny waist, and slowly drawing me into him. The fresh scent of the top notes of his manly perfume envelopes and invades my senses, and am I weakening at the knees at the heavenly fragrance of this divine man who has finally, once again found us. He quickly senses that my strength is dwindling and as he does, I find myself supported firmer within his cosseting embrace. With a few ounces of my stamina still remaining, I rise onto my tippy-toes, and gaze lovingly up at him. He looks down upon me, and our eyes meet. While I drink in his warming beauty, and when I see myself reflected within the delicate pools of his steely blue irises, I feel as if I am about to do one of two things; either faint in his muscular arms or lift off to an undiscovered level.

He nuzzles into my tresses breathing in the bouquet of my being. We are now oblivious to the world that is hurriedly scurrying around us; we linger like this for some time. As our souls silently join together, these most precious of moments turn into present memories in the making. On hearing the soothing tones of his velvety voice murmur, "You're so petite, my angel from above."

I shiver but not from the elements, but from the warmth of his love. My lips now trembling, I reply, "Am I?"

"Yes, Helena, you are." He soothes, "You... You, feel so, so delicately, fragile with in my arms."

With his words filtering fast into my heart, I now know that I am not going to pass out, and that if it was at all physically possible, I would freely elevate. Now safe in his arms at last, a place I never, ever want to depart from, I bury my head into his firm chest, and he wraps his coat around me. While the December snowflakes cascade around us and Mother Nature dusts us with her virginal beauty, the noise of the world around us fades into a non-existence. Replete in his company, I quietly say one word to him and that word was – breakable.

"Never," he tenderly soothed. "You will never fragment as long as we are together."

"You promise me, Darius? You promise that you will never let me shatter again?"

Stroking my hair, he took a sigh, and then with such honesty in his voice, he affirmed to me, *"I promise."*

JL Thomas' websites where you can keep informed as to when Book two, 'Quantum Entanglement' of 'The Gentle Dominant' series will be released.

https://twitter.com/jl_author
https://uk.pinterest.com/jlthomasauthor1/
http://thegentledominantdariusandhelena.blogspot.co.uk/